D0913164

CAUGHT DEAD

Other Available Books by Dorothy P. O'Neill:

A Liz Rooney Mystery Series:

Seeing Red
Grim Finale
Final Note
Smoke Cover
Ultimate Doom
Fatal Purchase
Double Deception

Avalon Romances

Heart's Choice
Change of Heart
"L" Is for Love
Beyond Endearment
Heart on Hold

CAUGHT DEAD

•

Dorothy P. O'Neill

AVALON BOOKS
NEW YORK

Published by Thomas Bouregy & Co., Inc.
160 Madison Avenue, New York, NY 10016

Library of Congress Cataloging-in-Publication Data

O'Neill, Dorothy P.
Caught dead / Dorothy P. O'Neill.
p. cm.
ISBN 978-0-8034-7779-7 (acid-free paper)
1. Rooney, Liz (Fictitious character)—Fiction. 2. Women forensic scientists—Fiction. 3. Gang members—Crimes against—Fiction 4. Police—New York (State)—New York—Fiction. 5. New York (N.Y.)—Fiction. I. Title.
PS3565.N488C38 2010
813'.54—dc22

2010006236

PRINTED IN THE UNITED STATES OF AMERICA
ON ACID-FREE PAPER
BY HADDON CRAFTSMEN, BLOOMSBURG, PENNSYLVANIA

To Harrison, Barlow, and Adeline,
my third generation.

Prologue

State Senator Ernesto Ruiz, home from Albany for the weekend, settled his corpulent form into a leather chair and looked around the study of his recently purchased Manhattan town house.

The big mahogany desk, adorned with sterling silver framed photos of Gina and the children, the antique Persian rug on the gleaming hardwood floor, the handsome tapestry draperies drawn across the clerestory windows, and his college and law diplomas displayed on the walnut-paneled walls never failed to bring on a smile. The smile was not as much from satisfaction as gratitude. Yes, it was partly his own ambition and hard work that had gotten him all this, but only in the United States of America could ambition and hard work bring the son of poor Puerto Ricans out of a Manhattan *barrio* into a life once beyond his wildest dreams.

Only in this great country could he have become an important political figure. Only here could he buy a house in a fine neighborhood, big enough for his wife, his children, including the orphaned son of Puerto Rican cousins he and Gina had adopted at age seven, and also his mother, sister, and brother.

His one regret was that his father had not lived to see it all, for it was *Padre* who'd taught his three very young children of America's greatness. "You were born in a wonderful country where you can become anything you choose to be," he'd said in Spanish. "I regret that I did not learn correct English and make it my own language. This you must do, and you must stay in school and get as much education as you can to prepare yourselves for the opportunities."

They'd all listened—himself, especially. Heeding *Padre's* advice, he'd mastered English and made it his language. He'd studied hard and worked his way through college and law school. His younger sister and brother, Yolanda and Carlos, both finished high school and got good jobs, Yolanda as a hospital aide, and Carlos as a clerk in a florist's shop.

Now, look at the three of them—he a New York State senator, Carlos now manager of the florist shop, and Yolanda had risen to the position of supervisor before she quit her job to run the household. Gina, whose law-firm job left her no time for housekeeping, said they could never hire anyone to manage this big house the way Yolanda did, as well as care for his widowed mother, the children's beloved *Abuela.* Not that *Abuela* needed special care, Ernesto thought with a smile. Before coming to the States she'd worked as *nana* for the three lively sons of a wealthy Puerto Rican family. Now in her eighties, she was still as strong as a burro.

Abuela, who spoke little English, enjoyed knitting in her room overlooking Central Park, watching Spanish-language TV, or going for walks in the park when the weather was good. Of course Yolanda or Carlos always went with her, and sometimes one or more of the grandchildren. Thinking of the grandchildren's devotion to their *abuela,* Ernesto smiled. His daughters, Rita and Cheryl, sons Julian and Manuel, and Geraldo, the orphaned cousin, now his and Gina's third son—they all loved her.

But Ernesto recognized that it was his brother Carlos who was the most devoted, even more than their sister Yolanda. When Carlos was not at work, he would spend much of his time with his *Mamácita* in her room, talking to her in Spanish while she knitted.

It was sad that the man Yolanda would have married was killed in an automobile accident. As for Carlos, his pleasant, good-looking face, tall stature, and muscular build had attracted many women, but strong ties to his *Mamácita* left him little time for *amorío.* He too had not married.

Reflecting further, Ernesto felt thankful for Gina's national background. Like many Italian immigrants, her great-grandparents had come here in the early 1900s and very quickly became true Americans. A Puerto Rican wife might have wanted to live in a section of the city where people clung to the Spanish language and made no attempt to fit into the ways of this great country. He wanted his children to be real Americans. Having an Italian American mother had already helped to accomplish this.

His chances of marrying someone like Gina had been so slim that, even after twenty-four years of marriage, he sometimes asked himself how it had happened. It was pure luck. They'd met in the public library—he who drove a delivery truck by day and attended NYU at night, and she a daytime college student whose parents could afford to pay tuition. They married soon after finishing college, and both got student loans to see them through law school. Gina's parents disapproved of him at first, but he'd earned their respect.

Of course they'd had to postpone having their own family, but now their two daughters and two of their sons were as American as the Anglo friends they'd made in the private schools they attended. They were children any father would be proud of.

All except Manuel. This plaguing thought lurking in the back of his mind brought on a sudden frown. Countless times he'd asked himself why Manuel had turned out so different from the others. If one of them was going to be troublesome, you'd think it would be Geraldo, who could have already come under bad influences before he and Gina adopted him. But Geraldo was a good boy. Although he was not very smart in school, he'd never given them any worry.

Yolanda's voice from the doorway deepened the frown. "Ernesto, I've got dinner almost ready, and Manuel's not home yet."

Ernesto forced a smile. "It's his birthday. He knows you always cook what he likes best and bake him a birthday cake. He'll be home soon."

He wished he could be sure that Manuel would not skip

having dinner with the family on his eighteenth birthday. But both Gina and Yolanda had told him about Manuel's often coming home late for dinner and sometimes not at all.

Ernesto shook his head. Again he wondered why Manuel had been a difficult boy since early childhood—disobedient, rebellious, and disrespectful of his elders. No kind of discipline worked. In sixth grade he'd been expelled from the parochial school the children used to attend, and he'd constantly played hooky from public school. The private school the others now attended would not admit him. He'd made it into public high school but dropped out after two years. So different from his brother Julian, now in college, and his prep-school sisters, Rita and Cheryl, both good students. Even Geraldo, now seventeen and only in tenth grade, held back because he was a slow learner, did the best he could in school and never gave them any trouble.

Gina's brother, a psychiatrist, had tried to help with Manuel, but Manuel refused to cooperate. His attitude toward family members was hostile. *Abuela* was the only one he showed any respect. He seemed to enjoy visiting her room and listening to her talk, in Spanish, about her childhood in Puerto Rico. From this, Ernesto took some hope. A boy who spent time with his grandmother must not be all bad.

Yolanda's voice came into his musing. "Okay, I'll wait a few minutes before I put the food on the table."

A sudden thought convinced Ernesto that Manuel would not pass up his special dinner. There'd be presents to open, and the usual birthday card containing money. He had not yet given up thinking that Manuel's surly nature would change. The usual hundred-dollar bill with his birthday card might help.

At that moment he heard someone coming in the front door. Swiveling his chair, he called out. "Manuel?"

His son's voice sounded from the hall. *"Sí."*

The Spanish response did not surprise Ernesto. Gina had told him that lately Manuel had been speaking more Spanish than English. Although Ernesto had taken great care to make

English the family language, he'd also told his children not to abandon the language of their Puerto Rican forefathers. But it rankled him to hear Manuel speaking a language other than English in this American home.

"Come in here, son," he called.

Manuel slouched into the doorway. Ernesto noticed he had on a sleazy-looking black jacket instead of the fine quality brown leather one he'd gotten for Christmas. But it was the bright green and orange cloth sticking out of the pocket that brought a sick feeling into Ernesto's belly.

He recognized the green and orange cloth as a gang bandana, and he knew that if he could see the back of the black jacket, there would be the green and orange serpent—emblem of *Las Serpientes,* known as the Serps, a Manhattan street gang with ties to the Puerto Rican Nationalists.

Years ago, *Padre* told him about the radical Puerto Rican Nationalists and their attempt to assassinate American president Harry Truman. This had stirred feelings against the Nationalists that Ernesto felt to this day. He held nothing against the idea of Puerto Rico's becoming an independent nation, if that's what its people wanted, but only ten percent of the population was for it. Most Puerto Ricans were pleased with living in a United States Commonwealth as statutory citizens, even though they could not vote in U.S. elections like those who came to live in the States.

But this did not lessen Ernesto's sick feeling or his rising anger. He longed to grab Manuel by the neck of his sleazy black jacket and yell at him, *"So, you have joined the Serps! What would Puerto Rican independence mean to you, an American citizen?"*

Instead, he took a deep breath and quelled his anger. Were others in the family aware of this? he wondered. Had his time spent in Albany while the state legislature was in session made him the last to know that Manuel had joined a street gang? Later tonight, he would discuss this with Gina. Perhaps this was the first time Manuel had openly worn his Serps jacket.

But at least Manuel had come home for his birthday dinner. For a little while he'd be part of the American family gathered around the table in his honor. And at least he'd show his affection for his grandmother when he opened her gift to him. *"Gracias, Abuela,"* he'd say, giving her a kiss.

Yes, Ernesto thought, there might still be hope for Manuel. Before confronting Manuel about his affiliation with an organization that had once tried to kill an American president, he'd give him a chance to realize how lucky he was to be an American on this, his eighteenth birthday.

"Happy Birthday, son," he said.

Perhaps because the thought of his usual birthday money had entered his mind, Manuel gave an agreeable nod and turned to hang his jacket in the hall closet. During that moment Ernesto caught a glimpse of the detested orange and green serpent on the back.

They were all seated around the dining room table, Gina at one end, he at the other. Ernesto looked at each of them—on one side Yolanda, Carlos, Manuel, and *Abuela.* On the other side, Geraldo, Cheryl, Rita, and oldest son, Julian, home from Princeton for the weekend.

Despite lingering effects from the shock of discovering that Manuel now belonged to a gang with ties to the radical Puerto Rican Nationalists, Ernesto felt a sense of pride. Surely Manuel must feel it too, this belonging to a close-knit family in a country that was truly the land of opportunity. After he'd eaten his special dinner, after Yolanda brought his birthday cake to the table, and after he'd opened his gifts, especially the package from his dearly loved *Abuela,* Manuel would have a change of heart.

Now the moment came when the birthday candles were blown out, the slices of cake eaten, and all Manuel's gifts except the one from his grandmother opened. That morning *Abuela* had shown Ernesto and Gina a sweater she'd finished knitting for her beloved Manuel—cashmere, with a pattern of tan and brown diamond shapes. Gina called it an Argyle sweater. They'd agreed it was handsome, and Manuel would certainly put it on the minute he saw it.

Ernesto noticed *Abuela* watching, smiling, when Manuel opened the box containing the sweater. He knew she was waiting for Manuel's eyes to light up and to hear his loving *"gracias"* as he leaned over and kissed her.

Instead, Ernesto was shocked to see a scowl on Manuel's face and hear anger in his voice. "You're trying to make me look like a *gringo* nerd!"

Ignoring the tears springing into *Abuela's* eyes, he grabbed the sweater out of the box and flung it down onto the table with a snarling, "I wouldn't be caught dead wearing this!"

Within seconds he was out of his chair and out of the room, and sounds—first of the coat closet door and then the entrance door slamming—told the stunned, speechless family that he was out of the house.

Chapter One

Liz Rooney was enjoying her usual Saturday morning leisure when the phone rang. Unlike on most mornings, when she rushed to get ready for work, she'd made coffee in the makeshift kitchen of her one-room apartment and then gone back to her sofa bed with a mugful to watch TV news.

"Liz!" The caller was Sophie Pulaski, her best friend since first grade, now an NYPD officer. She sounded excited. "I gotta make this quick. I'm in my squad car at a homicide scene," she said. "Ike and Lou are on the case. They just got here. I know Ike will give you the details later, but this looks like the kind of murder you like to follow. I wanted to tell you about it so you can start figuring things out right away."

Liz's senses went on alert. She'd been following murder cases since her strawberry blond hair was in pigtails. Her father, recently retired from NYPD Homicide, always encouraged her to delve into them and try to come up with possible clues. In this he'd been joined by his close friend, Dr. Dan Switzer, New York City's medical examiner. Dan had given her a clerical job in his office after college, and since Pop and Mom moved to Florida, he'd become something of a proxy father.

But Manhattan's back-alley, drug-related killings didn't especially engage her. They were largely cut-and-dried. Her amateur sleuthing seemed a better fit for cases in which victims or perpetrators came from backgrounds where murders were rare and sensational, such as prominent political figures, show biz personalities, or widely known wealthy persons.

"Thanks, Sophie," she said. "What happened?"

"The body of a young man was found in an alley near the service entrance of a west side deli. He was stabbed in the throat. Evidently he's been dead for several hours—maybe since around one or two in the morning."

Liz shuddered. The many descriptions of murders she'd heard over the years had not desensitized her. The violent ending of any human life always disturbed her. It took a moment before she asked, "Any ID on the body?"

"Nothing's turned up yet, but from his clothes he looks upper-class," Sophie replied. "He has on a beautiful Argyle sweater—hand-knit, cashmere. Look, I gotta go. Talk to you later."

Did Sophie think this case qualified because the victim was wearing a handsome sweater? Liz wondered. He could have stolen it. But Sophie had joined her too many times in following sensational homicides not to recognize one they'd both find interesting.

Suddenly she felt like someone with an intense thirst who'd been given a drop of water. She could only hope that Sophie would call her back soon and fill her in. Otherwise she'd have to wait for Ike to give her more details when he came over for dinner tonight. Fortunately, her good luck in digging up information had led to clues that had helped him solve recent homicides. Now even the DA had acknowledged her input as helpful, and Ike had become open to discussing cases with her.

It hadn't always been that way. Detective George Eichle—Ike to his friends—used to resent her interest in following homicides. When she accompanied Dan to crime scenes where Ike was present, he'd glare at her and snarl, "What are you doing here, Rooney?"—as if to say that if the medical examiner wasn't Pop's close friend, she wouldn't be there. But her nose for hidden clues gradually turned all that around, and their relationship went from rancorous to romantic.

Now they were planning a mid-February wedding—only a few weeks from now. She'd already moved some things out of her one-room apartment in Rosa and Joe Moscaretti's converted brownstone into the larger flat recently vacated by their other tenant. The new furniture she and Ike had recently bought had been delivered. Ike, who'd been renting a partially furnished apartment downtown near the Battery, wouldn't have to move anything except his clothes and computer.

Although they'd been tempted to move right into the ready-and-waiting apartment, they'd agreed to postpone that until after their wedding.

"Ever since I've lived in Rosa and Joe's building, they've been watching over me like I'm their own daughter," Liz had told Ike. "It's almost the same as having Pop and Mom living downstairs." She'd paused and laughed. "But I didn't give that too much thought till you and I began to get serious."

"Yeah," Ike replied with a rueful grin. "They've been chaperoning us for the past ten months. I guess we can put up with it for another few weeks."

Another few weeks. Ike and his partner, Lou Sanchez, had solved many a murder case in less time. Would they track down the killer of the man in the Argyle sweater before the wedding? she wondered. She couldn't picture Ike fully enjoying a week-long honeymoon in the Bahamas with the murderer still at large and another officer filling in.

As soon as she got more information about the victim, the sooner she could decide whether she should put her wits to work on the case. If it turned out that this was the kind of murder she was good at delving into, she'd do everything she could to help Ike wrap it up. She'd done it before; she could do it again.

Chapter Two

Ike phoned a while later. “I guess Sophie’s been in touch with you,” he said.

“Yes, she told me she saw you at the scene of a homicide this morning.”

She imagined Ike nodding his head, brushing back an unruly lock of sandy hair falling over his brow. There’d be a serious look in his hazel eyes. Although she hoped he might elaborate on what Sophie had told her, she wasn’t surprised when all he said was, “Right.” He disliked talking about his cases on the phone.

“Sophie thinks this is the kind of case I’m good at digging into,” she said, hoping he’d at least verify that.

He didn’t. “Okay if I stop by in a few minutes?” he asked. “I’ll fill you in then.”

It was almost lunchtime. A quick survey of the fridge came up lacking anything worthy of feeding Ike except the hamburger and salad slated for that night’s dinner. While she was asking herself if she could make it to the nearest deli and back with sandwiches before he arrived, a knock sounded at her door, followed by a voice.

“Dearie, I brought you a couple of slices of pizza pie I made for lunch.”

She opened the door to a smiling Rosa and the delectable aroma of fresh, homemade Italian cheese pie emanating from a covered platter.

“Oh, Rosa, thanks so much!”

From past experience, Liz knew that Rosa’s idea of a couple of slices would likely be two or three huge wedges. This wasn't the first time she'd been bailed out by Rosa in the culinary department. Sometimes she felt that Rosa might have some special instinct that enabled her to know when she should come to the rescue.

Coffee was ready when Ike arrived. She'd set up the old gateleg table Gram had given her to help furnish the apartment. Between castoffs from Gram's Staten Island house and what Mom gave her when she and Pop moved from the Island to Florida, this tiny place on the fringes of Gramercy Park was cozy and comfortable. In a way, she'd miss it when she and Ike were married and living in the larger apartment down the hall. This was where it had all begun for them.

Ike eyed the table and sniffed the aromas of coffee and pizza. "Lunch!" he said, giving her a kiss. "I was going to take you out for a bite."

"Nice thought, but thanks to Rosa, we can eat here. Besides, we couldn't talk freely about the case if we went out somewhere."

She carried the pizza, still warm from Rosa's oven, to the table, saying, "I want to hear all about this morning's murder."

Ike settled himself at the table with a nod. "The cops found a jacket in a nearby trash bin. Had a wallet in one of the pockets. We got full ID. They found a bandana too."

"A bandana? The kind gang members wear?"

Ike nodded. "And the jacket had the emblem of *Las Serpientes.*"

"The Serps!" she exclaimed. So, the victim was a gang member. She felt a pang of disappointment. On the list of cases she wasn't quite as savvy at following, street-gang killings were right up there with armed robbery and drug-related murders. Strange that the victim's wallet had been left near the scene, she thought. Positive ID of a body was usually the first step toward tracking down a killer. Maybe this wasn't gang related. Maybe it was a mugging gone awry.

Ike's next statement told her it wasn't. "We've ruled out

robbery," he said. "There were several tens and some singles in the wallet."

While she stared at him in puzzlement, thoughts of the victim's handsome Argyle sweater rushed back into her mind. She felt inclined to agree with Sophie—the apparel seemed to indicate a conservative, upper-class person. Worn by a member of *Las Serpientes,* known for its affiliation to the radical Puerto Rican Nationalists, it would be as out of character as a mink coat on one of the gang's female cohorts. So, who was this victim?

Ike must have seen the question in her eyes. "According to the ID in the wallet, the victim's name is Manuel Ruiz," he said. "When we followed through on it, we found out he's the son of State Senator Ernesto Ruiz."

Startled, Liz reflected on that. She knew that Senator Ruiz had been born to Puerto Rican parents in a New York *barrio* and had worked his way into the mainstream. He was now known for his ironclad American values and his opposition to radical causes, including the Puerto Rican Nationalist movement. Publicity about him depicted a large, loving, multigenerational family, a spacious home in one of Manhattan's upscale sections, and children in prestigious private schools, including one son in Princeton.

"How could a son of someone like Senator Ruiz get mixed up with a gang?" she asked. "Maybe the wallet found in the trash bin belonged to some other man named Manuel Ruiz."

Ike shook his head. "We went to the address given on the ID, and it was the home of Senator Ruiz. The senator and his wife told us their son, Manuel, left the house last night after dinner and hadn't returned. When we went over his bedroom, we found photos and other personal articles that left no doubt he was the murder victim. We picked up his fingerprints too, and while we were at it, we got prints from his brother Geraldo's schoolbooks. The two boys shared a bedroom."

"Did you get the prints of any of the other family members?"

"No. We'll do that when we go back to interview them. After we were done with the boys' bedroom, we took the senator and his wife to the morgue, and they identified the body."

What a terrible shock for them, Liz thought. Ike's next words told her he too empathized with the victim's parents.

"A birthday card was found in the victim's pants pocket with the name *Manuel* written on the envelope," he said. He paused, adding, "The card was signed, 'With love on your eighteenth birthday from Mother and Dad'."

Liz's imagination took off. "It was his birthday. Maybe the Argyle sweater he was wearing was a birthday gift. Maybe he wore it to a gang meeting last night, and the gang leader disapproved of it and ordered him to get rid of it, but . . ."

"But he refused?" Ike shook his head. "Even if wearing an Anglo-style sweater is a violation of gang rules, most likely continuing to wear it would be punishable by a roughing up, not murder."

"Of course you're right," Liz said. She paused, reflecting on the situation. "I wonder why the killer didn't take Manuel's wallet."

Ike nodded. "And removed any other possible means of ID from the scene too—the Serps jacket, the bandana, maybe even the sweater."

Puzzled, Liz replied, "It's strange that the killer or killers didn't do that. Maybe they heard someone coming and had to get away from the scene in a hurry, so they just dumped everything into the nearest trash bin and split."

A sudden thought popped into her mind. "What about the murder weapon?" she asked. "Was it found at the scene?"

"No. That was the one thing the killer didn't leave behind. There was a switchblade in the jacket, but it was clean. The amount of blood on the body indicated multiple stab wounds. We won't know for sure till after the autopsy if it was a knife or something else."

He checked his watch. "I have time for another mug of coffee, then I'll have to leave."

"Can you make it back here for dinner?" she asked.

"Yeah. We're going easy with the initial interviews. They'll be as short as we can make them."

She recalled they'd already taken the fingerprints of Manuel and Geraldo Ruiz. "Will you get the rest of the family's fingerprints tonight?" she asked.

"No. We're holding off on that for now. At this stage of the investigation we don't want the family to think any one of them is a possible suspect. Also, we don't want to risk having the news media get wind of it and blow it up into headlines and bulletins."

This case was beginning to sound like something she could get her teeth into, Liz thought. "Will you let me know how the interviews go?" she asked.

He flashed a grin. "Sure. Now that the DA has acknowledged your sleuthing talent, there's damn little I can't tell you."

Good enough, she decided. Not so long ago there was damn little he *would* tell her.

Chapter Three

By the time Ike arrived for dinner that night, the murder of State Senator Ernesto Ruiz's son, Manuel, was all over the TV news.

Watching while they ate, Liz noticed that the coverage, though constant, was still pretty thin. "I guess there's not much to go on yet," she said, as they viewed photos of the Ruiz family, dredged up from files, and listened to the commentary.

"Yeah, there won't be much more than this for now," Ike replied.

A group photo came onto the screen as the newscaster spoke, showing two pretty, dark-haired girls and a teenaged boy in the foreground. Behind them two swarthy, well-built youths flanked an elderly woman—most likely the grandmother, Liz decided. Four adults stood in the back row.

She recognized Senator and Mrs. Ruiz from newspaper and TV photos, but not the other two. "Who's that big man and the other woman?" she asked.

Ike quickly consulted his notebook. "Manuel's aunt Yolanda and uncle Carlos," he replied. "The aunt told me she's in charge of running the household."

"That must be a fairly recent shot. The children look fully grown. Can you tell which one is Manuel?"

Ike studied the photo. She knew he was trying to find a resemblance between the bloodied body he'd seen at the crime scene and one of the youths in the family picture. "I'd say he's the boy on the left in the second row," he replied.

The news commentator had started to identify each person in the photo. The well-built youth Ike had pointed out was, indeed, Manuel, standing with his brawny brother, Julian, and their grandmother.

"That's a pretty big family," Liz said. She looked across the table at Ike, shaking her head in disbelief. "How'd you ever interview them all in one afternoon?"

"We split them up and shared our notes afterward. I took the senator and his wife, two sons, and one daughter. Lou took the aunt and uncle, the grandmother, and the other daughter."

"All those people live in the same house?"

"Yeah—apparently they're a very close-knit family. Of course they were all in shock. We tried to go easy this time around. We only asked about Manuel—his activities, his friends, things like that."

She looked at him in expectation. "And . . . ?"

Ike took a bite of his hamburger. He was stalling, she decided. Something interesting must have come out of at least one of those interviews, and he was debating whether or not to hold off on letting her know.

"We're going to do another round of interviews with the Ruiz family in a couple of days," he said. "By then the autopsy results should indicate what kind of weapon was used in the stabbing, and if need be we'll have the house thoroughly searched."

Liz's senses quickened. "Are you saying the family might be withholding information?"

"Possibly," he replied. "Here we have eight people living in the same house as the murder victim. You'd think at least one of them would know about his gang membership, but when we questioned them about it, they all acted as if they didn't believe it."

"Well, did you draw any conclusions about individual family members?" She hoped she didn't sound overly impatient.

Again, Ike looked at his notebook. "Okay, I'll give you a rundown on the Ruiz tribe. I'll start with the grandmother. *Abuela,* they call her. Lou interviewed her because she's not fluent in English. But he said that even with his questioning her in Spanish, she seemed confused. One thing he picked up on, though—evidently she and Manuel were very close. It seemed as if he was her favorite grandchild. His murder appeared to leave the grandmother greatly shocked and grief stricken—more so than any other family member, Lou thought."

Most likely because of the grandmother's age, Liz decided. The rest of the family must be just as devastated but better able to control their feelings. "You said *you* did the interviews with the parents. . . ." she began.

"Right. They were relatively calm, considering. I got the feeling the senator still hadn't faced reality one hundred percent. During the questioning, the victim's mother jumped in with most of the answers."

Liz recalled seeing a head shot of Senator Ruiz's wife in a newspaper. She'd thought at the time that the dark-haired, dark-eyed Gina Ruiz was very good looking.

In the accompanying article, she'd learned that the senator's wife was an attorney, a third-generation Italian American, obviously as smart as she was attractive. Considering that, and the fact that the senator spent much of his time in Albany, Gina Ruiz would likely know more than Ernesto about what was going on in the household.

"This time around we just wanted to get a line on Manuel—how he did in school, who his friends were, the kind of boy he was," Ike continued. He paused. "Here's something I was going to hold off telling you till I looked further into it, but I might as well let you know now—Manuel was a problem kid since early childhood. Among other things, he was a high-school dropout."

"The parents told you that?"

"Not in so many words. It slipped out when they kept comparing him to their other son, Julian, apparently a model kid—a straight-A student from the word go, graduated from prep school with honors, and got into Princeton."

"So, they're accustomed to Manuel's being a problem.

Maybe when they find out he really was a Serp, it won't be too much of a shock."

"I got the feeling they might already know," Ike replied. "I can understand why they'd want to keep it quiet, but I expect it'll come out when I interview them again."

Liz recalled the group photo. "How about the brother who shared a room with Manuel? Did they say anything about him?"

"Geraldo? No, but I found out all about him when I interviewed him. He told me his natural father was the senator's cousin. Gina and Ernesto adopted him after both his parents died. He's in the same private school where the Ruiz girls go. And something else I picked up—his IQ isn't off the charts like Julian's. He's somewhat behind scholastically—seventeen in tenth grade, but, according to the parents, he's never been in any trouble at school or at home. Both Lou and I got the impression that he's a good kid."

"Manuel just had his eighteenth birthday," Liz said. "Being about the same age, he and Geraldo might have been pals. Was Geraldo terribly broken up?"

"Yeah, but no more so than the others. Julian, the Princeton brother, seemed angry as well as upset. I thought Cheryl, the fifteen-year-old sister, seemed overcome with grief, and Lou said the other sister, Rita, who's thirteen, was crying during her interview."

"What did Lou say about the aunt and uncle he interviewed?"

Ike consulted his notes. "Yolanda Ruiz and Carlos Ruiz. According to Lou, they were both visibly shaken up, and Lou said he noticed that the uncle seemed very concerned about the effect all this was having on the grandmother."

So many family members. Liz felt confused for a moment. "The grandmother," she said. "Is she the mother of Uncle Carlos and Aunt Yolanda and the senator too?"

"Right," Ike replied with an understanding smile. "It took some time for Lou and me to get them sorted out too. At first we thought Aunt Yolanda and Uncle Carlos might be man and wife, not brother and sister, but Lou got it all straight when he interviewed them. Neither of them was ever married, he said."

Recalling the family photos, Liz wondered why the aunt and uncle had remained single. Yolanda was a good-looking woman—pushing sixty, she judged. Carlos, probably a few years younger, had a bland, almost boyish face and a tall, robust build. The expression *gentle giant* came to mind.

TV coverage of the murder ended with the newscaster urging viewers to stay tuned for further developments.

"Will there be any new developments tonight?" Liz asked, pouring their after-dinner coffee.

"Not unless word gets out about Manuel's gang affiliation."

"Is that likely to happen?"

Ike nodded. "It wouldn't surprise me."

Routinely they took their coffee to the sofa and watched TV. Now, though, Liz thought of their future dwelling place down the hall, freshly painted by Joe, some of the furniture they'd just bought already delivered. Although they hadn't arranged everything yet, and the place looked a bit like a home-furnishings storeroom, their new living room couch was in place, and their lamps were unpacked and ready to shine on the new coffee table.

"Since there probably won't be anything else on about the case tonight, let's have coffee in our new apartment," she said. "We haven't had a chance to sit on the new couch yet."

"Good idea," Ike replied, picking up his mug. "I've been wondering if our elegant new couch is going to be as comfortable as your old sofa."

Their empty mugs had been on the coffee table for a while, and they'd agreed that the new couch had passed with flying colors, when Ike's mobile phone sounded.

He glanced at the caller ID. "It's Lou," he said, clicking on and launching into a one-sided, mostly monosyllabic conversation.

Lou wouldn't be calling unless there'd been a development in the Manuel Ruiz murder, Liz thought. Ike had mentioned the possibility of Manuel's affiliation with the Serps getting out.

Had it happened?

Chapter Four

Ike clicked off his phone, saying, "Manuel's gang membership just came out in a TV bulletin."

Liz sensed that he wished it could have been kept quiet until the investigation was further under way. Both he and Pop had told her that when a case developed sensational angles, it often became harder to solve. And news that a state senator's son belonged to a gang with close ties to a radical organization his father was known to detest was certainly sensational.

"Did some investigative newshound sniff that out?" she asked.

"Maybe," he said. The laconic reply told her he was mulling the idea over in his mind. She picked up their coffee mugs, and they headed down the hall to her TV.

"You said you thought the parents already knew about Manuel's gang membership, but I guess the whole family knows now," she said, listening to a commentator expound on the bulletin.

"Right. With this all over the TV news, if any of them didn't believe it, chances are they do now."

"Do you think others besides the parents might have known?"

"Yeah. At first I thought it was only Ernesto and Gina, but when Lou and I compared notes on the interviews, we both got the feeling the others could be holding back information too."

A look in his eyes suggested there was more on his mind.

"Do you think there's something else they're not telling you?" she asked.

He nodded. "They held back on the gang membership. That could mean there's other information they're sitting on."

"Any idea what?"

"Not yet, but maybe we'll find out tonight." He cast her a regretful look. "I have to leave. I'm meeting Lou at the Ruiz house."

For an unexpected round of interviews with a family whose secret is out, Liz thought. *Are there more secrets waiting to be revealed?*

Liz was getting ready to open her sofa bed, curl up under Gram's patchwork quilt, and continue watching TV, when Sophie phoned.

"I wanted to call sooner, but I was pretty sure Ike was there," Sophie said. "Then I heard the news about Manuel Ruiz belonging to the Serps, and I figured Ike would hightail it to the Ruiz house."

"You're right—he did," Liz replied. "He and Lou want to talk to the family some more." She told Sophie about Ike's initial interviews.

"When Ike questioned them about Manuel's being in the Serps, they pretended they didn't know?" Sophie asked. "Someone must have known. He has two brothers, doesn't he? Wouldn't they have picked up on it?"

"One of the brothers, Julian, doesn't live at home—he's at Princeton and only comes home for weekends," Liz replied.

"Okay, maybe he wouldn't know," Sophie said, "but how about the other one?"

Liz filled her in on Geraldo.

"If anyone knew Manuel was a Serp, it would be this adopted cousin his own age," Sophie declared. "They might have been buds."

Liz hesitated before telling Sophie what Ike thought about that. But more than once Ike had given her the green light as far as enlightening Sophie was concerned, and she'd never let them down. If a seasoned cop who'd originally caught the case now being worked by the detectives, and whose new husband was in NYPD detective training, couldn't be trusted to keep her mouth shut, who could?

"Ike thinks most of the Ruiz family might have been withholding that information, plus more," she said.

"More? Like what?"

"He said he doesn't know yet. It's a feeling he got during this afternoon's interviews."

"When Ike gets a gut feeling, he's usually on to something," Sophie replied. "Maybe it will come out in tonight's interviews." She laughed, adding, "Too bad Pulaski and Rooney, Private Investigators, aren't up and running."

Liz smiled at the reference to their longtime dream. Before Sophie Pulaski met Ralph Perillo in the NYPD Police Academy, and before NYPD Homicide Detective "Ike" Eichle decided that little redheaded Liz Rooney wasn't a thorn in his side, she and Sophie had talked about forming their own PI firm. With Sophie's police background and her own flair for ferreting, they were sure they'd be a huge success.

Now, with Sophie on the force and newly married to Ralph, and with Liz in the ME's office and with her own wedding to Ike coming up in February, the dream, though not completely dormant, had dwindled for the time being.

"But we don't have to be licensed PIs to follow this case and track down possible clues," she said.

"True. Especially you," Sophie replied. "Let me know if you come up with any ideas."

Later, in her sofa bed, Liz watched TV for a while. By now, coverage of Manuel Ruiz's membership in *Las Serpientes* dominated the news. She knew it would not have been such a big story if the murder victim wasn't a state senator's son.

Tonight's interviews with the Ruiz family members should be almost finished, she decided. Even if, as Ike suspected, most of them knew about Manuel's membership in the Serps, realizing that it was now common knowledge must have been a shock. Had this made anyone vulnerable enough for Ike and Lou to draw out the further information they believed was being withheld?

She turned the TV off and lay awake, asking herself exactly what the rest of it could be. In her mind's eye, she reviewed each family member in the photo she'd seen on TV, trying to figure out which ones might know something they were holding back.

The grandmother could probably be eliminated, she thought, and possibly the two young sisters. But if, according to Ike's hunch, some family members were, indeed, withholding information, that left Manuel's parents, his aunt Yolanda and uncle Carlos, and also Julian and Geraldo. All might be keeping something to themselves.

She recalled Sophie's agreeing that Geraldo, close to Manuel in age, would have been the most likely family member to know about Manuel's gang membership. Her imagination—Ike called it her *wildfire imagination*—went into action. What if Manuel had tried to interest Geraldo in joining the Serps? And what if he'd succeeded? Having *two* sons in the Serps gang would definitely be something the senator would want to keep quiet.

But suppose Geraldo had refused to join the Serps? Suppose he'd told Manuel that, like their father, he was opposed to the Puerto Rican independence movement and wanted nothing to do with any organization linked to the radicals who'd once tried to assassinate a United States president?

Wouldn't that have caused a rift between the two boys? Could that disagreement have turned a former comradeship into mutual dislike—perhaps even hatred?

Questions crackled into her mind like thunderbolts. Could Geraldo have had something to do with Manuel's murder? Was that the information binding the Ruiz family in a conspiracy of silence?

She didn't expect Ike to phone her that night with a report on the interviews. It would probably be late when he and

Lou finished up, and Ike would think she'd be asleep. As if she could so easily fall asleep with those startling questions stirring her mind. Most likely the questions had struck Ike's mind too. The need to discuss them with him would keep her awake, maybe for hours.

In her brief appraisal of Geraldo in the family photo, she'd noticed he was not as tall or as well built as Manuel and Julian, but he looked wiry. Was he strong enough to have overpowered Manuel in a struggle—perhaps the struggle that ended with Manuel dying from multiple stab wounds in his throat?

Thoughts of the stabbing reminded her that it had not yet been determined what sort of weapon had been used. She told herself it had to be a knife but not necessarily a switch-blade. Many men carried pocketknives, she thought, the kind with bottle openers and various tools on them. The murder might not have been premeditated. If Geraldo had done it, maybe he'd used his pocketknife in self-defense.

Suddenly she realized she was concentrating totally on Geraldo. Her imagination had run rampant, and the idea of ill feelings between him and Manuel had taken on an aura of reality. But those feelings could just as well have existed between Manuel and Julian. The Ivy League son could be as staunch a supporter of his father's views as was the adopted cousin. And Julian might have had a pocketknife on him too.

And so might Uncle Carlos and the senator, she thought. Even some women carried jackknives. Sophie had had one even before she became a cop. It had a tiny flashlight on it, as well as a small nail file and a screwdriver. When she and Sophie were locked in an old icehouse at a mountain lake resort last summer, that sharp little knife had helped get them out. She had no doubt it could also have been used as a weapon.

Now her imagination had all the Ruiz females carrying pocketknives!

But if one of them *had* stabbed Manuel, what would her motive have been? Liz asked herself. She decided to forget about motive for the moment and do some ruling out.

Again, she felt sure the grandmother could be eliminated. Although in the family photo she'd looked strong and healthy, she must be at least eighty. She couldn't imagine a woman of that age owning a pocketknife, much less plunging it into the neck of the strong, young grandson she dearly loved. Besides, the crime scene was nowhere near the Ruiz home. How would she have known that Manuel would be on that dark, deserted street, and how would she have managed to get there? No, she decided, the grandmother was definitely not the killer.

Following much the same logic, the chances seemed slim that Gina would have killed her son. Also, vivid as her imagination was, it couldn't create a convincing picture of either young teenaged sister stalking her brother on that dark street, knife ready for the kill.

That left Aunt Yolanda. At her age, she seemed as unlikely as Manuel's grandmother or mother to own a jackknife. Also the other common circumstances appeared to rule her out.

Liz was about to dismiss Aunt Yolanda as a suspect, when she remembered something. Aunt Yolanda was the family housekeeper. She'd have access to an array of knives in her kitchen.

With a start, Liz realized she'd come a long way from her original suspicions about Geraldo. If Ike knew, he'd laugh and tease her about her "wildfire imagination," she thought. Tomorrow, when they discussed this case, she'd skip over her far-fetched ideas and just ask him the question that had started her train of thought. *Could Geraldo Ruiz have had something to do with Manuel's murder?*

Chapter Five

Ike phoned before eight the next morning. "Hope I didn't wake you up," he said. "I know this is early for a Sunday, but I'm going to be busy for a while, and I wanted to set things up for us sometime today."

That sounded as if he and Lou hadn't completed their interviews at the Ruiz home the night before, Liz thought. They must need to finish up this morning.

"I'm awake and having coffee. When do you think you can get here?"

"How about between twelve-thirty and one?"

"Perfect."

At that hour Ike would be hungry. She was going to ten o'clock Mass with Rosa. There'd be plenty of time after the service to get some food in. She knew Ike would suggest going out for lunch. Although she felt thankful that he wasn't the "What's for lunch?" type, going out to eat would mean waiting till they got back to her apartment before they could talk freely about the case. Besides wanting to hear the details about last night's interviews, speculation concerning Geraldo Ruiz had left Liz with a craving for answers.

When Ike arrived, Liz tried not to fire questions at him before he was barely through the door. Instead, she told him she'd made Reuben sandwiches.

"Great, I'm starved," he replied. "And I guess you still have a couple of bottles of that German beer I brought over the other night."

They sat down at the gateleg table. She held off asking

him about Geraldo until he'd taken a few bites of his sandwich and a generous quaff of beer.

"Last night when I was thinking about the case, it occurred to me that Manuel and Geraldo might have been good friends. . . ." she began.

"Yeah, I guess so—they were the same age," he said. He paused, casting her a puzzled look. "I thought you'd be all over me right away about the interviews."

"Of course I want to hear how they went, but there's something I want to run by you first."

"About Geraldo?"

"Yes. What if Manuel tried to get him to join the Serps, and Geraldo said no way and came on strong expressing his feelings against the Puerto Rican Nationalists? That would have made Manuel angry, wouldn't it? And couldn't it have caused bad feelings between them?" She paused. "But maybe you already thought of that."

He cast her an approving look. "No, we didn't, but we should have. Manuel's trying to get Geraldo to join the Serps, and Geraldo's refusal stirring up bad blood between them—that's a definite possibility. And it ties right in with what we found out this morning."

Liz felt a twinge of excitement. "Oh? Are you saying Geraldo could have had something to do with Manuel's murder?"

"Not so fast, Redlocks," he replied.

She smiled, as she always did when he used this joking comparison to Sherlock Holmes. "But you said the idea of Manuel trying to recruit Geraldo into the Serps is a tie-in with what you found out during the interviews."

"You'll think so too, when you hear this."

She wanted to say, "So let's hear it," but she quelled her impatience, telling herself she should be glad Ike let her in on things, even though the information was sometimes slow in coming.

"With Manuel's gang connection all over the news, we hoped the family would be ready to loosen up and tell us what else we felt they were withholding," Ike said. He shook his head. "Last night we interviewed everyone in the family, but nobody was talking. It was getting late, so we knocked off and went back this morning. We didn't get anywhere until we talked with Rita, the thirteen-year-old daughter."

"Isn't she the one Lou told you was crying during her first interview?"

"Yeah. She seemed very vulnerable, Lou said. We both thought if the whole family was withholding information, she might be the one who'd eventually break down. We were right. This morning she told us that something bad had happened at Manuel's birthday dinner. After that we questioned everyone else again and finally got the whole story."

Liz could no longer restrain her impatience. "When are you going to let *me* in on 'the whole story'?" she asked.

"Don't get your Irish up," he replied with a grin. "I thought you'd like some background first."

"Thanks, it was helpful, but . . ." She looked at him expectantly.

"Okay," Ike said. "They all described a scene at Manuel's birthday dinner Friday night, when he opened the box containing the gift from his grandmother. She'd knitted him a cashmere Argyle sweater."

"The same sweater he was wearing when his body was found?"

"Right."

"You said you thought Manuel and his grandmother were very close, so I guess he put the sweater on and told her how much he liked it," Liz replied. "But what about the bad scene they all described?"

"Manuel didn't thank his grandmother or put the sweater on. He took one look at it, yanked it out of the box, flung it down on the table, saying he wouldn't be caught dead in it, then stormed out of the house."

Liz stared at him in astonishment. "Talk about irony!" she exclaimed. "And how could he be so cruel?" She paused with a puzzled frown. "But if he wasn't wearing the sweater when he left the house . . ."

Ike finished the question. "How come he had it on when his body was found? At first we thought he might have felt remorseful about hurting his grandmother's feelings and came back later to put the sweater on and tell her he was sorry. But once we got the family members talking, we began to have second thoughts. They all told us the same thing. The grandmother was devastated. She kept saying she'd never knit anything again. After Manuel stormed out of the house, Uncle Carlos helped her up to her room, and everyone else followed. They all stayed with her, trying to comfort her, till Aunt Yolanda said she'd get her into bed. What made us believe that Manuel hadn't returned to the house and made peace with his grandmother was how they described her the next morning. They all said she was still just as sad and tearful the following day as she was the night before. They mentioned that she wouldn't touch the knitting project she'd started—a scarf and cap for Rita. Yolanda told us they'd all agreed to leave the yarn and needles out on *Abuela's* chairside table instead of putting them into her knitting basket."

"Hoping she'd eventually go back to work on the cap and scarf?"

Ike nodded. "But Yolanda said she wouldn't even look at them."

"If Manuel had come back to the house, put the sweater on, and gone to his grandmother's bedroom to patch things up, she would have picked up her knitting, all smiles, in the morning," Liz said. "At least until she found out what had happened to him."

"Aunt Yolanda said the sweater was on the dining room table when she cleared it, after she put the grandmother to bed." Ike continued. "Rita and Cheryl were helping her, and they corroborated this. They said they didn't know what to do with the sweater, so they put it back into the box and left it on the table. Yolanda said that when she went to set the table for breakfast the next morning, the box was there, but the sweater was gone."

The look on his face told Liz he was as puzzled as she, but thoughts of the grandmother's distress lingered, overcoming her puzzlement.

"Poor old lady. What a terrible shock it must have been when she found out about Manuel's death and how he died. How did she seem during her first interview, just after the family was told about the murder?"

"According to Lou, she appeared dazed and kept mumbling something in Spanish—*'capturado muerto,'* I think he said. Anyway, he said it means *caught dead.*"

Caught dead, Liz thought, recalling what Ike had told her about Manuel's reaction to the Argyle sweater. Apparently the grandmother knew enough English to understand those harsh words, spoken in lieu of the warm thanks she'd expected. *"I wouldn't be caught dead wearing it!"* The irony must not have been lost on her.

"So, Manuel didn't come back for the sweater," she said. "That means someone took the sweater to him."

Ike nodded.

Liz's imagination flared. She pictured a struggle in that dark, deserted alley, the sweater being forced onto Manuel—its fine yarn and intricate pattern soon soaked with his life's blood.

Moments later, imagery gave way to reality. *Whoever took the sweater out of the house must have killed Manuel. How could that person be anyone* but *a member of the Ruiz family?*

Chapter Six

In a flash, Liz felt sure she was seeing it all clearly. Geraldo might be the tie-in to the information finally dragged out of the family members—such as trying to keep Manuel's gang membership and the ugly scene at the birthday dinner to themselves. And if they were aware of a rift between Manuel and his adopted brother, they might have tried to keep that quiet as well.

She became aware of Ike's gaze fixed on her and the suggestion of a smile on his face. "See what I meant about a tie-in?" he asked.

She nodded. "It sure sounds as if they suspect Geraldo and they're protecting him. I'm surprised they'd do that, when . . ."

"When Manuel was their flesh-and-blood son, and Geraldo was adopted?"

"Yes. And considering the possibility that Geraldo might have turned against Manuel, do you think he could be the killer?"

"It's way too soon to call him a suspect," Ike replied. "But did you get a good look at that family photo on TV? In a struggle between Manuel and Geraldo, Manuel looked like he'd come out on top with one arm tied behind his back. When I saw Geraldo in person, I was even more certain he'd be no match for Manuel."

"Yes, I noticed," Liz said. "But I thought Geraldo looked strong and wiry. Maybe he had some moves—karate or something."

"Good thought. I'll dig into it." He paused. "I know it's

beginning to look as if someone in the Ruiz family might be implicated in Manuel's murder, but there are other angles we need to look into."

Other angles—like what? The instant she asked herself the question, the answer seemed obvious. *The Serps.* Manuel could have had an enemy within his gang. But whatever turned up, she hoped the case would be solved well ahead of her wedding day, only a few weeks away. As modest as the wedding was to be, there were details to be finalized. She couldn't give them her full attention while trying to figure out who'd killed Manuel Ruiz.

They finished eating. Ike helped her clear the table. They took everything to the tiny area with a small sink, fridge, and stove screened off from the rest of the room. It was no wonder she wasn't much of a cook, Liz thought, setting their empty beer glasses down on the crowded counter Joe Moscaretti had squeezed in for her. When she and Ike moved into their apartment down the hall, she'd have a real kitchen. No excuse not to have the big fridge well stocked and tasty meals prepared on an updated stove. Gram had already given her some good recipes, including Irish stew—Ike's favorite. But she couldn't keep from hoping that Rosa would continue to share her scrumptious Italian dishes.

They left the makeshift kitchen and sat down on the sofa. "You're quiet all of a sudden," Ike said, settling in among Gram's needlepoint pillows. "I guess you've been thinking about the case."

She smiled. "No, I was thinking about how well fed you're going to be when I have a decent kitchen."

He gave her a kiss. "You haven't heard me complain. Before you came into my life, it was nothing but takeout and frozen dinners."

He'd been quiet too, she thought. "You've hardly said a word for a while yourself," she said. "I'll bet you're the one who's been thinking about the case."

"You're right," he replied. "I was reviewing that new twist you came up with."

"About Geraldo and Manuel?"

"Yeah. I was thinking, how could Geraldo, or anyone else for that matter, have known where Manuel went when he took off that night? Nobody followed him—in every interview we were told the exact same thing. The whole family went up to the grandmother's bedroom right after Manuel left the house."

"Well, they've been holding back all along," Liz replied. "Maybe one of them *didn't* go up to the grandmother's room."

"Took off after Manuel to see where he went, then came back for the sweater?" Ike gave a nod. "I guess that could have happened."

He always considered her ideas—even the wild ones, Liz thought. That was one of the many reasons she'd fallen in love with him. But she didn't think the idea she'd just presented to him could be called wild.

When Manuel stormed out of the house, he'd probably headed for the Serps' hangout, not realizing that he was being tailed. She imagined a shadowy figure following him to his destination, then hurrying back to the Ruiz house, waiting until everyone was asleep, then taking the sweater and sneaking out again. She pictured Manuel, walking the dark streets homeward, unaware that someone was lying in wait for him.

Now her wildfire imagination was up and running. Manuel, taken by surprise, had been dragged into the alley before he could bring out his switchblade to defend himself. She pictured the assailant's weapon being plunged into his throat, the Serps jacket torn off, and the Argyle sweater forced onto his bleeding body.

She shuddered, unable to believe that any member of the Ruiz family would be capable of such brutality. Maybe Manuel had had a violent clash with a Serps member that night. But how would a gang member have gotten hold of the sweater? And would a gang member have thrown the Serps jacket and all means of ID, plus cash, into the nearest trash can for the police to find?

It looked as if Manuel's killer was not a savvy criminal but a novice, she thought. That description could fit any member of his family.

Ike's voice came into her musing. "It's a nice day—sunny and not too cold. Let's drive up to Central Park and go for a walk."

He was full of surprises, she thought. They hadn't done much walking together, anywhere. A stroll in Central Park sounded positively romantic.

"Just give me a couple of minutes to change my shoes and put on my mittens," she said.

Ike parked his car. Hand in hand, they started off along one of the park's walkways.

The pleasant day had brought many others to the park, she noticed. Young families, some with babies in strollers, teenagers, elderly people, and couples like themselves walked along the paths or rested on benches.

It had been such a long time since she'd been in the park, she'd almost forgotten how countrylike many of its areas seemed. Even on this winter day, vehicular traffic on the adjacent street was barely visible through the leafless trees and shrubbery. After they'd walked for a while, she thought if she could erase the sight of buildings towering above the treetops, she'd feel as if they were miles away from Manhattan.

"Let's sit here for a couple of minutes and take in the view," Ike said, guiding her to a vacant bench flanked by tall shrubs and overlooking a grassy slope.

She snuggled next to him on the bench. "This was a great idea," she said. "Why haven't we done this before?"

"I guess we should have," he replied.

She noticed he was looking carefully at several people seated on a bench a good stone's throw away. *Scrutinizing* would better describe it. Ike wasn't one for obviously staring at women, but Liz checked the bench for flashy females anyway.

Seconds later she believed she knew why Ike had suggested a walk in Central Park. Even at a distance she recognized the people on the bench from the TV photo. The women were Aunt Yolanda Ruiz and *Abuela.* With them were Julian and Uncle Carlos.

Discussing Geraldo's possible involvement in Manuel's murder must have given Ike some ideas, she decided. He knew the location of the Ruiz town house, across from the park, and he'd probably found out that, on afternoons when the weather was nice, family members regularly escorted the grandmother there for a stroll.

Ike caught her looking toward the bench and must have realized she'd figured it out. "Yeah," he said with a sheepish grin. "I was hoping Geraldo would be with them today and I could get a look at him while he's off guard."

So much for a romantic walk, she thought. "Well, at least you can observe Uncle Carlos and Julian," she said. As she spoke, she did a little observing for herself. College student Julian, wearing blue jeans and a Windbreaker-type jacket, had an athletic build. He looked much better able to win in a struggle with Manuel than Geraldo. Uncle Carlos, in neat black sweats trimmed with white, again impressed her as a bland, mild-mannered man with a strong physique. Even though he might be in his early fifties, a man as fit as he would have no trouble overpowering Manuel, she thought.

Just then her senses went on alert. Two men with camera equipment had suddenly appeared and approached the group on the bench. One camera was already in action, zeroing in on the grandmother.

"Paparazzi!" Liz exclaimed. "Why can't they leave a bereaved family alone?"

Ike muttered something under his breath. She hoped he wasn't thinking of intervening. She could almost see the coverage on TV and hear the commentary—an NYPD detective trying to stop two harmless photographers from making a few bucks.

She needn't have been concerned. In the next instant

Uncle Carlos leaped to his feet Seconds later one of the photographers lay on the ground along with his camera, and the other was backing away.

Liz held back an audible cheer. Ike cast an approving grin toward the scene, saying, "Uncle Carlos is pretty quick on the draw!"

Moments later, while the dazed photographer was still supine and the other obviously reluctant to tangle with the big man in the black sweat suit, Uncle Carlos turned, took his mother's hands in his, and drew her up from the bench. The others got to their feet, and, without so much as a backward glance, the whole group hurried off, taking a walkway leading out of the park to the street.

"Sorry I brought you out here under false pretenses," Ike said. "I should have told you what I was up to."

"Why didn't you?" she asked.

"I wanted you to think of it as a fun idea that had nothing to do with my work," he replied.

She laughed. "It was fun anyway. I liked seeing Uncle Carlos giving those insensitive photographers what they deserved."

"Me too." He gave her a light kiss. "I promise, in the future we'll get in some one-hundred-percent fun walks."

She peered through the trees toward the street. "Can you see the Ruiz house from here?"

Ike shook his head. "No, it's in the other direction, but it's fairly close." He paused. "I wish you could see the inside of it. I'm no interior decorator, but even I knew it's done up like something out of one of those fancy home magazines."

"I suppose the kitchen is wall-to-wall granite," Liz said.

"Yeah, and Yolanda has all kinds of antique cooking utensils hanging on the walls—old potato mashers, eggbeaters, ice picks, rolling pins—things like that. She told me she's been collecting them for years."

"Oh, that sounds interesting. Gram has a bunch of old stuff like that in her basement. Maybe I should ask her if we can have them to decorate *our* new kitchen."

"Keeping up with the Ruizes—all except the granite," Ike replied with a grin. He glanced at the pathway. "Do you want to walk some more before we go back to the car?"

"Sure. I can fire questions at you just as well walking as sitting," she replied, getting to her feet. "Like, what's the next move?"

"Tomorrow we should have an idea what was used in the stabbing," he replied. "After that we'll have the Ruiz house searched."

She'd followed enough murder cases to know that even when a killer washed a bloody weapon and believed it was clean, often minute traces of blood could be found on it when it was examined in the police lab.

While they walked, she thought about that, and a puzzling question came to her. If Manuel's killer was a member of his family, wouldn't the murder weapon have been disposed of—thrown down a sewer, maybe, instead of being brought back into their home?

She asked Ike about that.

"It could be something that family members are accustomed to seeing in the house," he replied. "A letter opener always on the hall table, for example, or a fancy metal nail file—part of a dresser set belonging to one of the women or girls."

"I get it," Liz said. "If it turned up missing, there'd be talk, and you and Lou might hear about it and get suspicious."

"Exactly."

"But don't you think at least one family member might have an inkling that one of them is a suspect?"

"That's possible, of course. But it's too soon to call any one of them an actual suspect."

"Oh, I forgot, the current term is *person of interest.*"

He smiled. "Right. Lou and I were careful during our first interviews not to imply in any way that we thought Manuel's killer could be one of them."

"But after you get the report on what kind of weapon was used in the murder, and the police start searching the house, they'll *all* know you think someone in the family is the killer."

"It had to happen eventually," he replied. "It will be interesting to see what reactions we get. Maybe it will tip someone's hand."

He slowed his pace. "Shall we head back to the car? I know your folks usually phone you at around five on Sundays."

His thoughtfulness was another trait she loved. She nodded. "Yes, I'd like to get home soon."

"We'll get back to your place in plenty of time, and after we've talked with them, we'll go out somewhere for dinner," he said.

"A romantic walk in the park and dinner out too?" she joked.

"I'm making up for tomorrow," he replied. "It's going to be a busy one. I might not get to see you."

She understood. Tomorrow, autopsy reports would be coming in, with indications of the weapon used in Manuel's murder. Ike would have an idea of what had been used, and most likely he and Lou would conduct a search of the Ruiz house.

But she wouldn't have to wait for Ike to fill her in on that. Working for the medical examiner who also happened to be Pop's close friend and her proxy father had many advantages. Tomorrow, Dan would tell her what kind of sharp object had been plunged into Manuel Ruiz's throat.

Chapter Seven

The next morning, when Liz passed Dan Switzer's office on the way to her workstation, his door was open, and he was at his desk. She knew he'd been watching for her when he called out, "Good morning, Lizzie. Come on in here for a minute."

That might mean he had a line on what kind of weapon had been used to kill Manuel Ruiz, she thought. "Good morning Dan," she replied, looking at him every bit as expectantly as she had when she was a kid, waiting for him and Pop to fill her in on the details of a homicide.

"I got a brief rundown from Ike on the Ruiz murder," he said. He gave a knowing grin. "I guess he told you all about it, and you've started tracking down the killer."

She nodded. "But I can't do any serious tracking till I know what kind of weapon the killer used."

"That's what I wanted to speak to you about," Dan replied. "I'm waiting for the final report. It should be in at any minute. I'll let you know as soon as I get it."

"Thanks, Dan." She started to turn away and proceed to her workstation, when his phone rang.

"Hold on—this might be it," he said, picking up the receiver.

A moment later he looked at her and gave a nod. She waited while he scribbled a few words onto a notepad. It could not have been much more than a minute, but it seemed an interminable time before he hung up the phone and handed her his notes.

"There you go, Lizzie," he said. He paused and smiled.

"But I know my handwriting isn't what it should be. I guess I should tell you, in my preliminary examination I found the stab wounds in the victim's neck inconsistent with the blades of commonly used knives or household items such as letter openers, scissors—things like that. Further examination indicated that the punctures were made by a round, sharply pointed object like an auger."

Liz recalled Pop's workbench in the garage of their Staten Island house. When she was a child he'd told her the names of all the tools in the big wooden box he'd made himself, and he'd described their functions. She remembered once watching him bore a hole in a heavy leather belt. "This tool is called an auger, Lizzie," he'd said.

Now she shuddered and tried to brush away the gruesome image of such an implement being rammed into Manuel Ruiz's neck. Like most households, the Ruiz home would surely have a toolbox with hammers and screwdrivers, she thought. All the family members had probably used those at one time or another. Augers weren't as common, but it was quite possible that their tool kit contained one.

"An auger's not the only possibility," Dan continued. "The report also says the punctures could have been made by a Phillips screwdriver or some kind of stiletto."

The household tool kit would certainly include a Phillips screwdriver, Liz decided. But a stiletto? The word had a cloak-and-dagger connotation, she thought with a frown. Who in the Ruiz family might possess that kind of weapon?

Dan must have noticed the frown. "You seem puzzled, Lizzie," he said. "I guess you're thinking a stiletto, or something like it, isn't an item you'd find in the average home, but I wouldn't rule out finding one in the Ruiz household."

That sounded as if Dan shared Ike's suspicion—and hers too—that someone in the Ruiz family had something to do with Manuel's murder. How had Dan picked up on that? If he and Ike had discussed the possibility, wouldn't Ike have told her that?

But now Dan was explaining what had led him to suspect

Ruiz family involvement. "Ike called me at home early Saturday morning to tell me about the murder and to say he was on his way to the morgue with Senator and Mrs. Ruiz to identify their son's body," he said. "I know both the senator and his wife personally, so I went in, hoping my presence might be helpful. Of course they were in a state of shock, and they blurted out some remarks that didn't make any sense at first. I noticed they seemed very confused about the sweater he was wearing when he was brought in. The senator mumbled something about its being Manuel's birthday, and Mrs. Ruiz remarked that the sweater was a gift from his grandmother, and she muttered something like, 'We all saw him rush out of the house without it.' "

"That made you and Ike suspicious," Liz said.

Dan nodded. "I figured there'd been some sort of trouble involving the sweater. Ike asked them a couple of questions. Their answers seemed vague to me, but, considering the shock they were in, I decided my suspicions might not be justified."

At that moment his phone rang again. "I'll talk to you later, Lizzie," he said, picking it up.

Liz headed for her workstation. Reflecting on what Dan had just told her, she considered striking Manuel's parents from her list of suspects. It certainly sounded as if they were as puzzled as she. On second thought, she decided she mustn't be too quick to eliminate Gina Ruiz and the senator. What if those remarks Dan assumed were made in a state of shock were deliberately calculated to throw anyone who heard them off track?

But Ike had heard the remarks too. She wished she didn't have to wait till tonight to discuss it further with him, as well as the evidence concerning the murder weapon. She would have liked to give it all more thought, but her morning's workload kept her too busy.

By noon, Liz was more than halfway through her morning projects. It was time for a lunch break. She usually went out to eat with three other women on Dan's clerical staff, but since it was a cold, blustery day, she decided to order in.

The elderly man who delivered her coffee and BLT on whole wheat from a nearby café seemed intensely interested in Manual Ruiz's murder, and he must have decided there was no better place to get information about it. Even before he set the bag down on her desk, he started making comments and asking questions.

"How about that Puerto Rican senator's son being bumped off? And how about him being in with them Serps, when everyone knows his father's against Puerto Rican independence? If you ask me, one of his own gang done it. Maybe the kid kept it secret who his old man is, and they found out."

And then, like others who assumed that, because she worked for the medical examiner, she viewed all the corpses, he asked, "Is it true his throat was slit?"

Telling him her job didn't entail spending time in the morgue would have disappointed him, she felt sure. Resisting the urge to make his day by fabricating a gory description for him, she merely nodded and paid the bill.

Turning to go, the man added, "You know, maybe it wasn't one of them Puerto Rican gangsters done it. Maybe it was someone from a rival gang. Them punks been fightin' and killin' each other since way back. If this one wasn't a senator's son, you wouldn'a heard nothin' about it, if you ask me."

She wasn't asking him, but his last statement reflected her own conclusion, Liz thought, watching him shuffle toward the elevator. And if the Argyle sweater hadn't been on Manuel's body when he was found, she might give some credence to the rest of what the old man had said. But except for the Ruiz family, who else but she and the detectives knew about the ugly scene at Manuel's birthday dinner? And who but one of the family would have wanted to force him into the sweater?

Had he been stabbed before or after the sweater was on him?

Before, she decided. He would have put up too much of a struggle otherwise.

Unless he were outnumbered!

That thought gave rise to a possibility she hadn't considered. Could two or more family members have joined forces? After a few moments of trying to figure out which ones might have been cohorts, she shook her head. It was hard enough to picture one family member killing another. Even her wildfire imagination couldn't handle the idea of two or more being involved.

Her thoughts returned to the murder weapon. Dan would have notified Ike and Lou about his conclusions by now. After they got a search warrant, they'd probably spent the morning looking all through the Ruiz house for an auger, a Phillips screwdriver, or a stiletto. Ike had seemed sure that if a family member was involved in the murder, the weapon would not have been disposed of. She recalled what he'd told her, his hunch that it was likely an item family members were accustomed to seeing in the house. The killer would want to avoid any questions about its sudden disappearance; thus, Ike believed the weapon would have been cleansed and returned to its usual place.

That made sense, she decided. She didn't have to stretch her imagination to picture Uncle Carlos remarking that the Phillips screwdriver was missing or Senator Ruiz saying he couldn't find the auger. But she couldn't imagine anyone asking, "Where's the stiletto?"

Whatever suspicious items Ike and Lou found would now be in the police lab, undergoing tests for traces of blood. They would probably have found an auger and a Phillips screwdriver in the Ruiz house—but a stiletto or something like it? She shook her head. What might there be in the Ruiz home answering that description?

The answer came in a flash when she remembered Ike's telling her about Yolanda's collection of antique kitchen utensils. *An ice pick!*

Chapter Eight

Liz felt even more impatient to discuss the case with Ike. He'd said he'd call her during the day, but, knowing he didn't like to talk about cases on the phone, she knew she'd have to wait till dinnertime to question him.

When he called, his voice sounded cheerful. Maybe they'd found the possible murder weapon, and maybe it was the ice pick. Would she be out of line if she casually mentioned Yolanda's culinary antiques? That way he might give her a hint to sustain her till she saw him tonight.

While she was considering that, he told her he'd be at her apartment at around six, and he'd bring takeout if that was all right with her.

"Sure," she replied. "I haven't planned anything. I was going to stop at the market on my way home."

"Okay then. What'll it be? Chinese?"

"Sounds good. We haven't had Chinese for a while."

Before she could get in a word about Yolanda's antique ice pick, he'd said good-bye.

Did the news media know about the search of the Ruiz home? she wondered. Probably some reporters and cameramen would have been hanging around there when the police vehicles pulled up and officers and detectives entered the house. That might have alerted them to possible Ruiz family involvement in Manuel's murder and set off a firestorm of speculation. If so, there'd be something on the news about it. When she turned on her TV news channel, shots showed police vehicles outside the Ruiz home. The search must be in progress now, she decided, and if, as Ike had mentioned, fingerprints were also being taken, would reporters have somehow gotten wind of that?

Just then a commentator reported that further interviews were being held, and some personal effects of the victim were being returned to the family. The possibility of Ruiz family involvement still remained strictly within NYPD Homicide. Plus herself, Liz thought with a smile.

The media might not have caught on yet, but the family would have to be pretty dense not to realize why their home was being subjected to a police search and why they were being fingerprinted. How had they reacted to the obvious fact that detectives believed the murder weapon might be somewhere in the house and one of them involved in the murder?

Her thoughts returned to Yolanda's ice pick. She felt sure Ike and Lou had found it, but if it tested positive for blood, that wouldn't necessarily make Yolanda the killer. Anyone in the family could have taken it down from its hook and returned it after scrubbing off the blood.

Again she found herself unable to imagine any member of the family going through that macabre routine, much less carrying out the gruesome killing.

Her phone rang at that moment. It was Gram, temporarily diverting her mind from murder to marriage. "I've just about finished the alterations on your wedding gown, dear," she said. "When can you come over to the Island for a final fitting?"

"How about Saturday morning?"

"Great," Gram replied. "I'll make your favorite mushroom-and-barley soup for lunch, and we'll have a nice visit. I want to hear your ideas about the murder of Senator Ruiz's son. It's my personal opinion that someone in a rival gang did it. Those gangs are always at each other."

Liz finally said good-bye, thinking how lucky she was to have a loving grandmother who was also an expert seamstress and cook—and as hooked on homicides as she was. She felt sure she'd inherited her passion for solving murder cases from Gram, along with hair Gram was determined would stay red as long as she could make it to Nick's Crowning Glory salon.

And how lucky too, she was to have a best friend like Sophie, who'd offered her the bridal gown worn by both her and her mother, saying it was supposed to be good luck to wear a happy bride's wedding dress.

"In this case, it's *two* happy brides," she'd said. "I'm bigger than you, but with a few tucks here and there, it'll fit perfectly."

If a trophy were being offered for the most economical wedding on record, this one would be the winner, Liz decided. Not having to buy a gown was only part of it. Although the guest list was small, and Sophie and Ralph their only attendants, they'd talked about holding a reception at an upscale catering hall. But when Mom and Pop came to Staten Island soon after being told of her engagement, they and Gram had made a joint proposition she and Ike couldn't turn down.

"Your mother and I could throw you a lunch or dinner reception at a fancy catering hall, with an open bar, a live band, and a five-tier wedding cake, or we could give you the equivalent cash outlay for whatever you want to do with it," Pop had told them. "It's up to you."

While they were still too surprised to reply, Gram had jumped in. "I could handle a small reception—say, twenty-five or thirty people—in my house. And if you had the wedding ceremony around two in the afternoon, that would make the reception too late for lunch and too early for dinner. You could get away with light refreshments, like Champagne and finger food, and I'll make you a beautiful wedding cake."

Money in the bank versus a few expensive hours of dining, dancing, and cutting into a multitiered cake that cost more than two weeks of Chinese takeout was no contest!

Gram's house wasn't what you'd call spacious. but, like many houses built in New Dorp during the 1920s, it had a good-sized entrance hall, living and dining rooms adjoining through a wide archway, and a sunporch along one side. There'd be ample space for the number of guests Gram visualized.

Mom had remarked that if she and Pop had waited another year to get married, they could have had their reception in Gram's house too. "But your grandparents were living in a small apartment at the time," she said. "We had a nice dinner for our families and friends at an Italian restaurant on New Dorp Lane."

She'd smiled. "Little did we know that twenty-five years later we'd be attending our daughter's wedding reception in her grandmother's house."

And giving the bride and groom a sizable nest egg, Liz thought with a small pang of guilt. Although Pop's NYPD retirement pay and Mom's pension from the New York City school system allowed them a comfortable living, they were far from wealthy. She and Ike had expected to help defray the wedding expenses, but Pop wouldn't hear of it.

After she'd said good-bye to Gram, Liz wondered again about the Ruiz family's reaction to the search of their home. It was difficult to imagine one of them as Manuel's killer. The time would drag until tonight, when she could talk everything over with Ike.

"I got General Tso's chicken and vegetable lo mein and egg rolls," Ike said, coming in with bags of takeout. On his way into the kitchenette he glanced at the gateleg table Liz had set up for dinner, as usual.

"I know you're itching to get into the case," he said. "Give me a couple of minutes to take off my coat and wash the city dirt off my hands, and I'll help you get everything into bowls and onto the table. Then we can talk."

The sooner they sat down to eat, the sooner they'd start discussing the search for the murder weapon and everything else, Liz thought. She generally set her dinner table properly, but tonight . . . "Let's skip putting everything into bowls," she said.

Ike slid out of his coat, casting her a surprised grin. "Take the cartons to the table and scoop everything straight out onto our plates? Isn't that one of my old bachelor habits you want me to break?"

"Not exactly," she replied, watching him wash up at her tiny sink. "Using cartons on the table instead of bowls is all right once in a while. It's the scooping everything out of the cartons straight into your mouth that I object to."

He laughed and gave her a hug. "Yeah, I'll admit that's not what you'd call refined, but I know you don't approve of putting takeout cartons on a dinner table either. How come that's okay with you tonight?"

"I don't want to waste time juggling dishes and talking about the food," she replied, taking the cartons to the table and motioning for him to be seated. "I want to hear how the Ruiz family reacted to the search and what you found. Dan told me the murder weapon could have been an auger or a Phillips screwdriver or something like a stiletto."

"We found several possible weapons," he said, spooning portions of rice and General Tso's chicken onto their plates.

"Did you find anything resembling a stiletto?"

"Yeah—including an old ice pick from Aunt Yolanda's collection."

She took a deep breath.

"You thought of that, didn't you?" he asked.

She nodded. "But all of a sudden I'm finding it hard to believe any one of them would have killed Manuel. It seems so out of character for any member of such a close family. Sure, they all must have been angry when he left the house after breaking his grandmother's heart, but . . ."

"One of them could have been a lot angrier than the others but kept it bottled up till it finally exploded," Ike said. "I've seen that in more than one homicide case."

But in this case someone would have had to be enraged to the point of insanity to murder a son, a brother, or a nephew, Liz thought. According to what the family had told Ike, when Manuel rushed out of the house, nobody followed him. They all went up to the grandmother's bedroom instead. Even if the enraged one slipped out of the bedroom unnoticed, Manuel would have had too much of a head start to be tailed.

Certainly Manuel would not have told his family the location of the Serps' hangout or the route he took coming from or going to his gang meetings. So how could it have been one of them who'd sneaked out of the house with the Argyle sweater, who'd lurked in a dark alley off a deserted street near the Serps' hangout, waiting to vent a smoldering fury?

A possible answer flashed into her mind. Despite her growing reluctance to believe that anyone in the Ruiz family was the killer, the possibility took her straight back to her starting point—her thoughts about Manuel and Geraldo. At one time, likely they were good friends. Suppose Manuel had succeeded in getting Geraldo interested in joining the Serps. Suppose Manuel had taken him to some Serps meetings before Geraldo decided not to join. Geraldo would know where the hangout was and also the route Manuel took on his way home.

"What's going on in that steel-trap mind of yours?" Ike asked.

When she told him, he nodded, indicating he'd considered that.

"It will all come down to the fingerprints on Manuel's birthday card and envelope," he said. "Of course Manuel's fingerprints are on both, and also his mother's, indicating she was the one who bought the card and handled it before giving it to him. But besides Manuel's prints and Gina's, there's a third faint set that we hope can be lifted."

"The killer's prints!" Liz exclaimed. "They might be Geraldo's!"

Ike nodded. "Possibly. But here's another angle. The senator told us there was a crisp, new, hundred-dollar bill with the card. We didn't find it. The killer must have taken it."

"Even if those extra prints can't be lifted, the prints on that bill could solve the case," Liz said.

"Yeah. Too bad that C-note is long gone. Any prints on a brand-new bill would be few and clear."

Liz helped herself to another portion of lo mein and did some speculating. What if it turned out that those prints on the birthday card and envelope weren't Geraldo's but the senator's? Wouldn't that indicate that he had taken the hundred-dollar bill? But why? And was it even possible that one of Manuel's parents could be his killer?

Unthinkable, she decided. Both parents could have handled the card and bill before the bill was put into the envelope, and Manuel could have removed it himself. But where would he have put it? Could he have spent it? Ike said Manuel's wallet contained only smaller bills. But why would one of Manuel's parents take back the birthday money? Why would *anyone* take it yet not steal the bills in his wallet? She shook her head in puzzlement.

Ike's voice came into her thoughts. He'd changed the subject to the search he and Lou had made of the Ruiz home.

"The whole family was present," he said. "Everyone's staying home from school and work till after the funeral. Needless to say, nobody was pleased about the search, especially the senator and Uncle Carlos. They insisted on knowing what we were looking for. We told them we weren't sure, which was pretty close to the truth."

"Did they see what you took?"

"No, it would have hampered the search to have them following us around. We had them stay in the senator's study with an officer."

"You know that as soon as you left, they checked to see what was missing," Liz said. "Aunt Yolanda probably noticed right away that her ice pick was gone."

"We assured them they'd get everything back in a day or so," Ike replied. "Anyway, the body's being released the day after tomorrow. They'll be too busy with funeral arrangements to worry about a few gadgets."

Ike often attended the funerals of unsolved-murder victims. Clues could sometimes be picked up by scrutinizing the mourners, he'd told her. Not long ago he'd taken her to one. Maybe he'd take her to this one too. "When's the funeral—do you know?" she asked.

"Yeah," he replied. "Thursday afternoon in the Ruiz family's church. I'd like to take you with me, but with all the city and state government officials expected to be there, the pews will be packed and attendance restricted. Of course the news media will cover the funeral, but only a few journalists will be allowed in. No cameras, and they'll have to stand in the rear."

Liz thrust away her disappointment. "I'm surprised that any media people will be allowed into the church at all," she said.

"Only a handful of journalists from newspapers that supported Senator Ruiz in his campaign for the state senate," Ike replied.

"Do you think the Serps will show up and try to get into the church?"

"They'll be there. The senator gave the okay for them to attend. We expect they'll show up full force."

"I'm surprised about that too," Liz said. "You'd think the senator would have them banned from the church."

"We were told he doesn't want to provoke an incident." He gave her a regretful look. "I'm sorry I can't take you with me, Liz."

"Well, I shouldn't expect to tag along every time you go to a funeral," she said. She suppressed a sigh. "But I would have liked to observe the family members during the service."

"Hey, that's *my* job," he replied. He looked at her for a moment. "Tell you what," he said. "A friend of mine from the *New York Post* is one of the approved journalists. I'll arrange for you to stand in the back of the church with him. Sorry you can't sit with me, but at least you can observe the family on their way out."

She smiled. "Thanks—that'll be great." She eyed his empty plate and the nearly empty food cartons. "Are you ready for coffee and dessert?" she asked. "I have ice cream to go with our fortune cookies."

"Yeah, let's see what messages Confucius has for us tonight."

He read his message first and handed it to Liz with a grin.

She read it aloud. "Your life's journey will soon be taking you in a new direction."

"How did Confucius know we're getting married?" she asked with a laugh. "Let's see what mine says."

She broke open the cookie and scanned the message. "It says, 'A new friend will guide you to where you want to go.' "

Ike put on a fake frown. "Since you want to go in the same direction as me, *I'll* guide you." He paused, adding, "Otherwise, this new friend had better be female!"

After Ike left, Liz thought about their fortune-cookie messages and laughed. Ike's sense of humor was one of the many traits that made her love him.

She fell asleep with the hope that Manuel Ruiz's murder would be solved before they headed in their "new direction" together.

Chapter Nine

When Liz turned on the TV news the next morning, it struck her that coverage of the Manuel Ruiz murder differed from previous cases she'd followed. The closest to anything sensational had been the announcement of Manuel's affiliation with *Las Serpientes.* There'd been very little harassment of the family by reporters and photographers. Though a discreet smattering of journalists were camped outside the Ruiz town house around the clock, waiting to interview anyone coming or going, it was not a media circus. She also wondered why TV news directors and newspaper columnists had not followed their usual procedure of seeking out and hounding friends and acquaintances of Manuel for relevant or irrelevant background details.

While she brewed coffee and toasted a bagel, she tried to figure out the reason for this lack of media frenzy. Because the young man so brutally slain was a New York State senator's son, the case had touch of celebrity status. It surprised her that it wasn't getting the big play given to recent cases she'd followed—like the murders of the country music star, the declared presidential candidate, and the Park Avenue countess.

Maybe it was a political thing, she decided. Since his election, Senator Ernesto Ruiz had become very popular with members of both parties. The press was probably being less aggressive out of deference to him and respect for his family.

But if the media ever got wind of what had happened at Manuel's birthday dinner, the press would be onto the family like a plague of locusts. Everyone, from the grandmother to the thirteen-year-old sister, would become fair game.

Not much chance of that, she thought. It had taken the combined efforts of skilled detectives Ike and Lou quite some time to get any information out of the Ruiz family. It wasn't likely any one of them would suddenly open up to a bunch of reporters.

A few minutes after Liz arrived at work, Sophie phoned. "Ralph's on duty tonight," she said. "Is there any chance we could get together for dinner?"

"Maybe," Liz replied. "I haven't talked to Ike yet today, but we don't have anything special on for tonight. I know he wouldn't mind if we skipped seeing each other. When he phones, I'll ask him and get back to you."

Ike generally called her during the afternoon, but that day he surprised her by phoning a few minutes after she and Sophie had said good-bye.

"You're early today," she said.

"Yeah. I wanted to let you know we're working late tonight. Do you think you can live without seeing me till tomorrow?"

She laughed. "I'll try. Matter of fact, Sophie just called. Ralph's on duty tonight, and she wants me to have dinner with her, so it'll work out okay." She paused. "Did something new come up in the Ruiz case? Is that why you're working late?"

"I'll tell you all about it tomorrow," he replied.

During the morning Dan stopped at Liz's desk on his way to the elevator. "Did Ike tell you that Manuel Ruiz's body is being released tomorrow and the funeral's Thursday?" he asked.

"Yes. Could I take some time off to go to it?"

Dan nodded. "Of course. It's at two, I heard. Take the afternoon off, Lizzie."

She smiled. "Thanks. Ike said if I could go, he'd take me to the church. He said it's going to be restricted, but he'd arrange for me to stand in the back with a friend of his who's a reporter."

"Good. That way you'll be able to get a good look at the family when they leave the church. There's a lot to be learned from facial expressions."

As he turned to leave, he cast her a teasing smile, saying, "I ran into Ike this morning. Looks like he's bearing up pretty well for a man about to give up the freedom of bachelorhood."

Where had Dan run into Ike? Before Liz could ask him, he was on his way. At this stage of the case, it wasn't likely that Ike would have been in the morgue today. But Dan occasionally went to the police lab. Maybe that's where they'd met up. If so, that might mean Ike had the results of the testing for blood on the possible murder weapons.

She remembered that Manuel's birthday card was also in the lab, being tested for fingerprints. Maybe he had those results too, although, if the prints were blurred, it could be a long, painstaking job.

Of all the nights for Ike to be working late, she thought. She'd be wallowing in speculation until tomorrow.

She called Sophie's cell phone to tell her she was clear for dinner. "Where shall we meet?" she asked.

"I've been thinking about that," Sophie replied. "Instead of going to a restaurant, let's eat at my apartment. With me married and you engaged, we don't get much chance to hang out anymore. Seems like ages since we've put our feet up and let our hair down."

"Sounds good. I'll stop at the market on my way over, and—"

"Oh, don't bother doing that," Sophie replied. "I did food shopping last night, and I have jumbo shrimp and a bunch of other stuff in the fridge."

"Okay. We can put together Gram's recipe for shrimp Creole."

"Great. I might be a little late getting home, so don't come straight from work. Come at around six-fifteen."

"Fine. That'll give me time to stop at my place and have a look at my mail. See you later."

Lunchtime came. With the weather sunny and not very cold, eating somewhere a short walk from the building would be a good idea, Liz thought. Her three co-workers—Michelle, Lawanda, and Eileen—agreed. They headed for a café a few blocks away.

The four of them had been eating lunch together often during the two years that Liz had worked for Dan Switzer, and they'd become good friends. Liz had told them about her penchant for following murder cases as well as her history with Ike. They loved it when Liz confided that the man she and Sophie Pulaski used to call Detective Sourpuss turned out to be the sweetest guy she'd ever known.

They knew Sophie from the pre-Ralph and Ike days, before Sophie went into the NYPD. Back then, she and Liz frequently grabbed fast food and took in a movie after work. Sophie had sometimes met Liz in the medical examiner's offices beforehand and had gotten to know the three co-workers.

"How's Sophie doing?" Michelle asked, after they'd settled themselves at a booth in the café and ordered.

"Fine. Enjoying work and married life. Did I tell you her husband's in detective training?"

Michelle nodded. "Yes. The two of you will both have real-live detective husbands. That's neat."

"It sure is," Lawanda agreed. "You'll be closer than ever."

"When you see her, tell her hello for us," Eileen said.

"I'll see her tonight," Liz replied. "We're having dinner at her apartment. Ike and Ralph are both tied up, so it'll be just us girls."

At that moment she noticed a fleeting look pass among the three. She couldn't define it. For a moment she felt puzzled, but it was forgotten when a waitress came with their food.

While they ate, the talk centered on Manuel Ruiz's murder. Like the elderly man who'd delivered lunch the day before, her three friends thought the killing was gang-related.

"Maybe he strayed onto the turf of a rival gang once too often," Eileen suggested.

"Or maybe he never let his own gang know his father was Senator Ruiz, and—" Lawanda started to say

Michelle broke in. "And when they found out, they eliminated him. I've heard that the Serps are mixed up with those crazy Puerto Rican Nationalists. Would they allow someone into their gang whose father is a state senator always speaking out against them?"

The elderly deliveryman . . . her three co-workers . . . even Gram. Liz felt sure there were many others who believed this was a gangland murder. Without knowing about the incident at Manuel's birthday dinner, no one else had reason to speculate about members of the Ruiz family. That included the media. Investigative reporters were probably working feverishly to unearth a possible link between *Las Serpientes* and Manuel's murder. If or when they found something that seemed to apply, there'd be sensational headlines and TV bulletins.

Back at her desk, Liz found a rash of work waiting for her. When she started attending to the last detail, it was almost five o'clock—quitting time. She noticed that Michelle had already shut down her workstation. Lawanda and Eileen were getting ready to close theirs.

"Looks like you three have hot dates tonight," she teased. Remembering that Eileen was married, she added, "All except you Eileen, unless it's your anniversary or something."

"Nothing so romantic," Eileen replied. "Walt and I are going shopping for a new washing machine."

A few minutes later she and the other two called good-bye to Liz and headed for the elevator. Liz finished her work and left soon afterward.

When she walked along her street and neared the Moscarettis' brownstone, she was surprised she didn't see Rosa at the window of what they called their front room. Rosa always watched for her, and by the time she entered the building, Rosa would be in the hall to greet her—like a mother, Liz often thought. Today there was no sign of her.

She picked up her mail; then, concerned about Rosa, she knocked on the Moscarettis' door. Joe answered.

"Hi, Joe, is Rosa okay?" she asked.

"She's fine," he replied. "She had to go out to the store."

On the way up the stairs to her apartment, she told herself it had been a lucky day when she answered the Moscarettis' ad in the newspaper. Sure, sometimes she felt as if they'd taken over where Pop and Mom left off, but during the year she'd lived in the apartment above Rosa and Joe, they'd become close friends.

She scanned her mail—the phone bill and a letter from Ike's parents in Syracuse. She sat down on the sofa and read the letter. They said they'd made reservations for themselves and Ike's great-aunt Hilda to fly down for the wedding.

That was a reminder that time was getting short. The wedding was only about three weeks off. Invitations had already been sent. Simple as it was to be, it still required planning, such as getting accommodations for Ike's parents and his great-aunt. With the wedding on Staten Island, it would be inconvenient for them to stay at a hotel in Manhattan. She and Ike had talked about getting them rooms in the Staten Island Hotel. They'd do that in the next day or so, she decided.

She checked her watch. Sophie had said get to her place at about six-fifteen. If she left in the next ten minutes or so, she'd be right on time.

Liz knocked on Sophie's apartment door. Sophie was a bit slow in answering it, but when Liz stepped inside, she was stunned to find herself surrounded by Sophie's mother and sister, Gram, Rosa, Eileen, Lawanda, and Michelle from work, and three friends from Staten Island.

A chorus of voices rang out. *"Surprise!"*

Liz's feeling of puzzlement vanished when she noticed the array of packages on the coffee table, done up in fancy wrapping paper and white ribbon. Dazed and delighted, she realized this was a bridal shower, and it was for *her.*

After a round of hugs, Sophie announced that food and wine were ready, buffet style, on the kitchen table. "We'll drink a toast to your marriage, and after we eat, we'll watch you open your gifts," she told Liz.

Gram had cooked her mouthwatering shrimp Creole, Mrs. Pulaski had put together a fancy salad and baked crescent rolls, and, for dessert, Rosa had made Italian pastries.

Looking at all the smiling faces surrounding her, Liz found herself misty-eyed. *What wonderful friends.*

While eating, she thought of Ike. How he would enjoy all this great food! Here she was, dining like royalty, while he'd probably grabbed a lousy burger somewhere.

The thought had barely entered her mind when another idea came to her. Plans for the shower must have been under way for quite a while, and, like everyone else, Ike might have been in on the surprise.

"Did Ike know about this?" she asked Sophie.

Sophie laughed. "Of course! He was in on it from the word go. He and Ralph didn't have to work tonight. The two of them are killing time together till after you've opened your presents. Then they'll show up here, and we'll feed them the leftovers."

Chapter Ten

Later, in the apartment that would soon be their home, Ike fingered a stack of fluffy beige towels and a shaggy beige and white bath mat. "These will go great with the tiles and paint color in our new bathroom," he said. "How come everyone knew what colors to get?"

"I told Sophie that Joe put in tan and white tiles and painted the walls beige," Liz replied. "She filled everyone in."

"I'm surprised someone didn't let the cat out of the bag about the shower. Didn't you have the slightest suspicion something was up?"

"Not a clue."

Suddenly she remembered the letter she'd received from Ike's parents. "I heard from your mother and dad today," she said. "They've made plane reservations for them and Aunt Hilda for the day before the wedding."

"We have to get moving on a place for them to stay," he replied. "We should call the Staten Island Hotel tomorrow and—"

"No, we won't have to. At the shower tonight, Sophie's mom told me she wants your parents and Aunt Hilda to stay at her house, which is huge."

He smiled. "Good for Mrs. Pulaski. That'll work out great. The hotel's on the other side of the island, and this way it won't be a hassle getting them from there to the church."

She nodded. "And with Pop and Mom staying at Gram's, we'll *all* be nearby. Well, except for you, of course."

She saw a sudden doubtful look come into Ike's eyes.

"I just thought of something," he said. "You'll be staying at Gram's the night before our wedding. With your folks taking over her guest bedroom, that means you'll be in that tiny room where Gram does her sewing. Last time you slept there, you were only a bridesmaid at Sophie and Ralph's wedding. But this time you're the bride. You'll have all your . . . your bride stuff in there, and Sophie will be in there helping you get ready, and probably your mother and Gram too. How are you going to manage in such close quarters?"

How sweet! He isn't worried about his *commute but about* my *comfort. Only a rare man would concern himself with such a detail.* Liz gave him a kiss, replying, "Gram's insisting on giving me her room for that very reason. She says it's only for one night and that the daybed in her sewing room is quite comfortable—which I can vouch for."

With a laugh, she added, "Thanks for being concerned about me, but maybe *I* should be concerned about *you.* Are you sure you can make it from Manhattan to the church on time?"

"Not to worry. Ralph swears he'll have me waiting at the altar long before your Pop walks you down the aisle."

With that evening's excitement, she'd almost forgotten Manuel Ruiz's murder. Now, thoughts of it began to return. She gave Ike time to look over more gifts before she switched the subject from bridal shower to bloodstained weapon.

"How did it go with the ice pick and the other things you got from the Ruiz house?"

He flashed a teasing grin. "I wondered how long it would take you to get back to the case."

"Am I some kind of freak, thinking so much about a murder when I shouldn't have anything on my mind but our wedding?"

He shook his head. "I love you just the way you are, Redlocks." He emphasized his words with a kiss.

"And, before you go wild with impatience—there were no traces of blood on any of the items we took from the Ruiz house," he added.

"So, what now?" she asked.

"We're still waiting for final results on the prints on the birthday card and envelope. Manuel's prints and his mother's have been verified, but there's that other set I told you about. They're unclear, but we're not giving up on them yet. A couple of experts have been called in to work on them."

Liz felt a shiver of anticipation. Whether or not those extra prints belonged to a Ruiz family member, it seemed likely that they were the killer's.

"What if the experts can't come up with a clear-enough lift?" she asked.

"There are items that haven't been tested yet. Long shots, but we can't overlook anything."

"Long shots? Like what?"

"Well . . . various items belonging to Manuel that the cops found in the trash bin."

"They'd be long shots, all right. Any new prints would be mixed up with Manuel's."

She felt a pang of discouragement. She wanted their honeymoon to be a respite for Ike, and, as much as she enjoyed delving into murder cases, for herself too. She wanted them to have nothing on their minds but each other.

"Do you think you'll have this case solved before our wedding day?" she asked.

He gave her a hug. "Maybe. But I've cleared it with the lieutenant. If we still haven't closed the case by that time, he'll assign someone to work with Lou while I'm gone."

A fleeting image crossed her mind of their leaving on their wedding trip with Manuel's murder unsolved. She pictured them in a romantic setting of tropical blossoms, sunshine, golden sands, and clear blue water, talking about fingerprints, weapons, and street gangs.

"If this isn't wrapped up before our big day, we'll have it on our minds during the entire trip," she said.

"We're putting in plenty of overtime on this," he replied. "There's a good chance it'll all work out before our wedding day."

Was Ike concentrating on something they hadn't discussed? With an inward sigh, Liz told herself that she shouldn't expect him to let her in on *everything.* She should consider herself fortunate that he was willing to tell her as much as he did.

That train of thought continued after Ike left. Usually, she fell asleep soon after hitting the pillow on her sofa bed, but tonight she kept turning the possibility of unshared information over and over in her mind. Did it have anything to do with the items Ike said hadn't been tested yet? If so, why did he say they were long shots? Why wouldn't they have been tested right away?

And what were those items? She recalled Ike's telling her that Manuel's Serps' jacket had been found in the trash bin, along with his wallet. Did he think something in the wallet might lead to a clue? Again, if so, why the delay in testing?

She decided that her imagination had put her onto the wrong track. If there was any real possibility of picking up clues from the items found in the trash, they wouldn't have been left untested all this time. First things first. The forensics experts were working hard to lift that important third set of prints on the birthday card. They had no time for long shots.

Chapter Eleven

On the way to work the next morning, Liz stopped in the lower hall to knock on the Moscarettis' door. When Joe answered, the aroma of a hearty breakfast cooking wafted from Rosa's kitchen. Liz knew she'd be invited to sit down and eat with them, and the prospect was tempting. Coffee and a bagel didn't hack it compared with bacon, French toast, and hash browns. But she didn't want to be late for work, especially when Dan was letting her take tomorrow afternoon off to attend Manuel Ruiz's funeral.

"Hi, Joe. I just stopped by to thank Rosa for helping Sophie put on the shower," she said.

A voice came from the kitchen. "Is that you, dearie?" In a moment Rosa appeared, all smiles, saying, "What a lovely time we had last night."

"It was wonderful. Thanks for making the cannolis."

"It was my pleasure, dearie. Can you come in and have some breakfast with us?"

Liz steeled herself against temptation. "You know I'd love to, but I should be getting to work. Thanks again for helping Sophie with my shower." She gave Rosa a parting hug.

After a busy morning at work, Liz went to a nearby restaurant for lunch with Lawanda, Eileen, and Michelle. Of course her three friends wanted to review the shower and get in a few comments about Ike, whom they hadn't met before last night.

"I'll never forget the look on your face when you realized what was happening," Eileen said.

"I was surprised, all right," Liz replied. "It was wonderful."

"Your fiancé seems pretty wonderful too," Lawanda said.

When Ike phoned during the afternoon, he'd barely said hello before he was lining up plans for the evening.

"I ran into Jim Valli today. You remember him, don't you? Used to be on the squad before he relocated?"

"Jim Valli? Sure. Pop thought very highly of him. Where did you see him?"

"He dropped into the station house to say hello. He and his wife, Connie, are in town for a couple of days. He suggested we get together for dinner tonight, and I said okay. I hope that's all right with you."

"Of course it is. It will be good to see him again and to meet Connie."

"Great. I told him I'd make a reservation somewhere. How about that place down on the Battery?"

She smiled. He'd picked a posh restaurant with food and ambience he knew she especially liked.

"You know I'd love to go there again," she replied.

"Okay then," he said." I'll go ahead and make the reservation and get back to Jim. I'll pick you up at your place at around six-thirty."

In the restaurant, they were seated at a table overlooking the Hudson River near the mouth of the harbor. Ike had made sure of that, Liz thought. He wanted her to be just as delighted with the view as she'd been last time they came here.

Jim's wife, Connie, an attractive, likable young woman, reacted to the ambience with enthusiasm. "This is wonderful," she said, looking out at the twinkling lights of passing vessels and, in the distance, a radiant Statue of Liberty. She turned to her husband. "Why didn't we ever come here while we lived in Manhattan, Jim?"

Ike laughed. "I'll get you off the hook, Jim. This place didn't open till after you moved upstate."

"Of course, or we'd have eaten here at least once a week," Jim replied. He scanned the menu, evidently noting the prices. "Or maybe not," he added with a grin. "What would you recommend?"

"We've only eaten here once," Liz replied, "but we both thought the fresh salmon steak with onion marmalade was absolutely wonderful. I'm going for that again tonight."

Ike nodded. "Me too."

"Sounds good," Jim said.

Connie agreed. They ordered.

"This is going to be a real treat," Connie said. "Restaurants like this don't exist in Scotch Corners."

"Do you miss the city?" Liz asked.

"Not really," Connie replied. "The advantages of small-town living far outweigh the disadvantages—right, Jim?"

"Right," he replied. "For one thing, there's a lot less pressure being a small-town sheriff than an NYPD homicide detective. Homicides are few and far between."

That remark sparked talk about New York's homicide rate. Soon they were discussing Manuel Ruiz's murder.

"It didn't get much coverage in our town newspaper, but we've been following it on TV," Connie said.

"It seems like a tough one," Jim added.

"It is," Ike replied. "We're still sorting out evidence and trying to pin down the murder weapon, but we're making progress."

"I have my own ideas about the murder weapon," Jim said. "Most likely you do too, Ike. I guess you've checked out the grandmother's knitting needles."

Liz only half heard Ike saying that they had. Her mind went on alert. A steel knitting needle plunged into Manuel's neck could have been as lethal as an auger, an ice pick, or any other potential weapon in the Ruiz household. Why hadn't she thought of that herself? She pictured family members gathered in the grandmother's bedroom after the ugly birthday-dinner scene. In her mind's eye, she saw the yarn and needles on the table next to chair where the grandmother did her knitting. With the entire family focused on her, someone could have removed a needle, unnoticed, slipped it into a coat pocket, and later sneaked out of the house to find Manuel.

She felt as if she were starting over, with Geraldo again her prime suspect. Her mind rekindled the thought that Geraldo's dislike of Manuel's gang activity might have turned violent. Also, Geraldo was probably the only family member who would know where to find Manuel. Was Geraldo the one who'd taken the knitting needle to use as a deadly weapon? After the fatal stabbing, had he brought the knitting needle back to the house to clean off blood and fingerprints before putting it back with the yarn and the other needle on the grandmother's table? *How grisly.*

Had Ike and Lou taken both knitting needles to the police lab, along with other potential weapons? Had intensive tests on one of the needles picked up incriminating evidence?

She told herself she should put those thoughts on hold and just enjoy the evening. It wasn't as difficult as she thought it would be. Light talk and laughter throughout the meal soon overshadowed her speculations. The evening ended with plans for another get-together the next time Jim and Connie came to New York, and their invitation for Ike and Liz to visit Scotch Corners.

"Who knows? Ike might like our little town so much, he'd want to become a county sheriff himself," Jim joked when they said good-bye.

"What a nice couple," Liz said on the way to her apartment. "I'd really like to see them again."

"Yeah, we should take them up on their invitation to check out small-town life," Ike replied. He cast her a grin. "Not that I have any idea of becoming a county sheriff. I've been working on big-city homicide cases so long, I know I'd miss them. And you would, too, wouldn't you?"

Liz nodded. "You know I would."

"That reminds me—Manuel Ruiz's funeral is tomorrow. You still want to go?"

Liz nodded. More than ever, now that thoughts of the knitting needles had entered her mind. She wanted to get a good look at Geraldo's face as the family followed the casket out of the church.

"Yes," she said. "Dan's giving me the afternoon off."

"Okay. The service is at two. I'll pick you up outside your building at twelve-thirty. We'll grab lunch somewhere and then head for the church. I spoke to my journalist friend at the *Post* and arranged for you to stand with him and some other newspeople Senator Ruiz okayed to attend."

While he sat in a pew as near as he could get to the Ruiz family, Liz thought. Did that mean he considered the family more of a source of suspects than the Serps?

"When the service is over, I'll have to get out of there on the double and meet Lou at the station house," Ike went on. "I'm slipping out a side door, and I won't be able to drive you home, but my friend, Sam, said he'd make sure you got out of the church okay. The Serps will be standing in the back of the church too, and . . ."

"And you think I wouldn't be able to resist the opportunity to dig for possible clues?" she asked.

He cast her a wry smile. "The idea occurred to me."

The idea might have occurred to her too, if Geraldo hadn't been on her mind. For a moment she'd considered mingling with the Serps after the service and asking a few questions but had decided against it. Sam, the journalist, would report her to Ike. She could almost hear him.

"I tried to keep an eye on her, but before I knew it, she was gabbing with the Puerto Rican gang."

Anyway, chances were close to zero that she could come up with something Ike and Lou hadn't already found out when they questioned the Serps. Again, she wondered if Ruiz family members were higher on their list of possible suspects than Serps members.

With a firm statement, she backed up her decision to stay clear of the gang. "I promise I won't say one word to any Serp."

"Good," Ike replied.

She sensed his unspoken words. Questioning the gang members might be risky. This was the first homicide case she'd tried to help him solve in which her snooping hadn't put her into danger, and he wanted to keep it that way.

But there'd be no danger in observing Geraldo's body language when the family followed the casket out of the church. *Not much excitement, either.* She tried to ignore a small pang of disappointment.

Chapter Twelve

Outside the Ruiz family church, Ike guided Liz through the crowd of reporters, cameramen, and telecasters, plus a horde of curious onlookers. It took only a flash of his badge to get them past the cordon of police.

Inside, in the back of the dimly-lit church, he introduced her to his friend, Sam Baumberg. "Take good care of her, Sam," he said with a grin. He gave Liz a quick hug, saying, "I'll see you tonight."

Watching him walk down the nave and enter one of the pews, Liz sensed he'd briefed his friend on her penchant for following murder cases and mentioned the resulting scrapes she'd gotten herself into. Clearly he felt confident that Sam would head off any potential trouble. But how could she get into any trouble when she'd promised Ike she wouldn't say one word to any Serp?

"Thanks for letting me stand with you, Sam," she said.

He nodded, giving her a friendly pat on the arm. "Glad to do it. Ike told me you're into following homicides."

While speaking, he glanced over her shoulder. Liz turned to see a group of about two dozen young men and several young women gathered in a back corner of the church, some fifteen or twenty feet away. Their ages ranged from late teens into the twenties. Were it not for their black jackets bearing the emblem of a coiling orange and green serpent, and their orange and green headbands, they could have passed for a group of students—friends of the young man whose body lay in the closed casket below the altar steps. But she sensed that the bond between them and Manuel Ruiz went beyond ordinary friendship. They were united in a way only they could fully comprehend.

"Senator Ruiz made a wise decision, not banning the Serps from the church," Sam said. "Sure, they're quiet now, but there could have been big trouble if they weren't allowed in. They're a volatile bunch."

As he spoke, the church door opened, sending a shaft of light into the semidarkness. A pretty Hispanic girl entered. Liz judged her age to be sixteen or seventeen. She stood near the door, hesitating, looking around—almost as if she were scared, Liz thought. Their eyes met for a moment so brief that it could scarcely be called a glance, before the girl looked away.

Apparently Sam had noticed the girl too. He seemed to be appraising her. Was he planning to work her into a column about misguided youth and gangs and the murder of an eighteen-year-old?

"Do you think that girl is a Serps member?" she whispered.

He shook his head and lowered his voice. "I doubt it. If she were, she wouldn't be wearing that brown coat—she'd have on her Serps jacket. And she wouldn't hesitate to go and stand with the gang."

Liz's glance returned to the girl. Sam was right. Instead of walking over to join the Serps, the girl now cast a furtive look in the gang's direction and remained standing near the door. Liz felt sure she wasn't a Serps member, and it seemed obvious she didn't want anyone in the gang to know she'd come to the funeral.

"It looks as if she's afraid the gang will notice her. Why?" she asked.

"She could be a girlfriend disapproved of by the membership," Sam replied. "Most gangs have strict codes about that."

"But, without Serps ID, how did she get past the police outside?"

"It's my guess she showed the Serps talisman—a silver

pin shaped like a coiled serpent. Members give them to their significant others. It would pass as Serps ID."

Liz turned that over in her mind. If the pretty teenager were a girlfriend rejected by the gang, she must have known they'd be hostile if they saw her there. They might even force her to leave. Why would an unaccepted girlfriend come to the funeral of a Serps member anyway?

A likely answer came in the next instant. *What if she were* Manuel Ruiz's *girlfriend?* That would explain everything.

At that moment the appearance of a priest signaled the start of the service. Liz saw the girl shrink into the shadows along the back wall of the church. Evidently she'd gone unnoticed by the Serps thus far. When the service ended, this sad, scared girl would probably huddle there till the gang left the church and dispersed.

She would have told Sam her idea about the girl's relationship with Manuel, but, from the start of the requiem, he seemed preoccupied. Maybe he too had drawn that possible conclusion. Whatever his mind was focused on, she didn't want to interrupt.

When the service was over and the casket borne toward the rear of the church, Liz concentrated on the Ruiz family members following it.

The senator and his wife appeared numb—as if they'd become anesthetized to the tragedy of their son's violent death. Yolanda's eyes looked red, and the faces of the two Ruiz daughters showed traces of tears. Carlos, escorting his black-veiled, audibly weeping mother, seemed mostly concerned about her. Both Julian and Geraldo looked grim, almost angry.

Disappointment swept over Liz when she studied Geraldo's face and failed to pick up anything indicating guilt or remorse. But that wasn't proof that Geraldo didn't harbor those emotions, she rationalized. Malevolent feelings toward Manuel could have overpowered all else.

She switched her attention back to the girl lurking in the shadows. When the pallbearers approached the door, the casket passed so close to the girl, she could have reached out and touched it. The look on her face wrenched Liz's heart. Now she had no doubt that this pretty teenager was Manuel's forbidden girlfriend.

Her imagination flared. What if the Serps suddenly discovered the girl? Surely they wouldn't accost her outside the church, in full view of police and TV cameras, but would they plan some future punishment?

The mourners following the casket out of the church obstructed her view of the assembled gang. That meant the gang's view was obstructed as well. Chances were they hadn't seen the girl yet, and now they'd be unable to see her through the crowd. She felt sure the girl would wait until all the Serps left the church and were gone from the area before she ventured to slip out.

Sam's voice came into her thoughts. "There's the governor—and the mayor too. Looks like every city and state official turned out for this. I hope that's some consolation for the senator and his family."

And for the girl who loved Manuel, Liz thought.

"Well, it looks like we'll be out of here in a few minutes," Sam said. He cast her a smile. "Did you pick up any clues?"

She returned the smile. "Just a few ideas. How about you? Did you get some good material for an article or a column?"

He nodded. "Plenty of human interest here."

They watched the pews emptying. Soon the last occupants were leaving the church, and the Serps were preparing to follow.

Watching the gang leave, Liz worried that one or more of them might spot Manuel's girlfriend on their way out. Some of the sheltering shadows had dispersed when the double doors were opened. Her eyes scanned the area near the door, and she glimpsed the girl, barely visible. Just as she sighed with relief, thinking it wasn't likely that any of the Serps would notice the small figure huddled against the back wall, she saw one gang member, a youth with mean, dark eyes and a deep scar on his chin, staring toward the area where the girl was standing. But when he continued on his way out of the church without hesitation, she thought he might not have seen her.

Sam must have noticed that too. "Looks like the blacklisted girlfriend might be home free," he said.

Liz gave a sigh. "Poor, scared little girl." She glanced out the doorway. Now that the Ruiz family, the governor, and other prominent persons had been whisked off in their limos, the crowd of curious onlookers in the street had dwindled. Media people were closing their notebooks, packing their cameras, and leaving the scene. Mobile TV trucks were pulling away. Of the large detachment of NYPD officers on duty earlier, only a handful remained, and all the orange and green bandanas and the black jackets with the coiled serpent logos had gone.

"Well, I guess that does it for my chances to pick up clues, so I'll be on my way," she said. "Thanks again for letting me stand with you, Sam."

"My pleasure." As Sam spoke, a man wearing a press badge similar to his approached him.

"Got a minute, Sam?" he called.

"Sure." Sam turned to Liz. "If you can wait till I've had a word with my colleague, I'll find you a cab."

"Oh, thanks, but I'll take the subway. It's right around the corner."

"You're sure?"

"Absolutely." She flashed him a good-bye smile.

Outside, she headed for the sidewalk, almost deserted now. That had been an interesting experience, she thought. Although her observations hadn't jelled into a possible clue, Sam had told her something she hadn't been aware of. Belonging to *Las Serpientes* went far beyond dedication to Puerto Rican independence. A member must also follow strict rules affecting his or her rights to a personal life. Why had the gang prohibited a romance between Manuel and his girlfriend?

The sound of a female voice from behind her interrupted her thoughts. "Miss . . ."

Liz slowed her pace and turned around. Out of the shadows of the church, in the early-afternoon sunlight, the sad, scared face of Manuel's forbidden girlfriend again touched her heart.

While wondering why the girl had followed her, Liz hoped a smile and a friendly response would ease her obvious anxiety. "Hello. I saw you at the service, didn't I?"

"Yes." The girl gave a furtive glance around. In a voice barely above a whisper, she said, "You're a reporter. I need to talk with you."

Seeing her standing with Sam and others wearing press badges, the girl had mistaken her for a reporter, Liz thought.

She started to explain, but a sudden thought changed her mind. A conversation with Manuel's girlfriend might shed some light on the mystery surrounding his murder. Recalling her promise to Ike, she rationalized that the girl was not a Serps member; therefore, talking with her would not be breaking that promise. She couldn't pass up the chance.

"Let's go somewhere for coffee," she said.

Chapter Thirteen

A wan smile crossed the girl's face. "Thank you, Miss."

Liz smiled in return. "My name's Liz Rooney."

"Mine is Dolores Otero," the girl replied.

Besides her soft, sweet voice, the girl's general appearance bore no resemblance to the stereotype depicted in old movies of the gangster's "moll" of Edward G. Robinson or George Raft. No heavy makeup plastered her pretty face, and her dark hair was not fashioned into an elaborate coiffure. Long, glossy, clean, and neatly brushed, it fell to the shoulders of her plain brown coat. Ironically, rebellious Manuel had fallen in love with a girl who looked as if she would fit right in with his parents' conservative values.

They found a self-serve café down the block. After they'd picked up their coffee, Liz saw an empty corner table where there'd be little chance of someone overhearing their talk. "How about over there?" she asked.

Dolores nodded. Liz noticed the quick glance she cast over her shoulder, as if she thought a Serps member might have spied her and followed her.

Liz recalled the scar-chinned Serp she'd noticed. "I'm not sure, but I don't think any of the gang saw you in the church," she said as they sat down.

Dolores' dark, expressive eyes studied her. "You . . . you seem to understand," she replied.

"About you and Manuel and the Serps' disapproval? I believe I do."

"But how did you know?"

"When I saw you come into the church, I thought you

looked scared, and I got the distinct impression you didn't want the Serps to see you. I put it together when the reporter I was with told me you might be a member's forbidden girlfriend."

Dolores nodded, brushing at her eyes. "You guessed right. Manuel was my boyfriend. We loved each other very much. . . ." She paused, her lips quivering. "The gang ordered Manuel to break up with me."

Liz held off asking why. She sensed that the details would come without prodding. The instinct proved to be right. Moments later Dolores took a deep breath and began to talk.

"You see, my brother belongs to the Montezumas. You probably know they're a Mexican gang who call themselves the Zumas, and they've been at war with the Serps for a long time."

Liz nodded. Like most New Yorkers, she had a smattering of knowledge about Manhattan's street gangs. This was a *West Side Story* thing. The Serps would not allow a relationship between one of them and the sister of a rival gang member. If Dolores' brother knew about it, he wouldn't permit it either.

She recalled Pop's telling her that the Zuma gang was among those involved in drug trafficking. If Dolores were aware that her brother's gang was into this criminal activity, it seemed unlikely that she'd want to discuss it with a reporter. So, what did she have on her mind?

Perhaps Dolores sensed the question. "I followed you out of the church because I believe you're going to write a story for your newspaper about Manuel," she stated. "I don't want you to write about a boy who rebelled against his father by joining a gang. There's much more to it than that."

Any guilt Liz might have felt for allowing Dolores to believe she was a reporter now weakened. The thought of getting a new slant on Manuel, and a possible clue to the mystery surrounding his murder, excited her. "I'll be interested in anything you have to tell me," she said.

Dolores took a sip of her coffee. "I guess I should begin

by telling you that Manuel and I met in high school. He was a year ahead of me, so we didn't have any classes together, but we met when we both joined the Spanish Club. The club was organized to promote an interest in Spanish history among Latino students. We held meetings every Friday after school." She paused, her eyes lighting up for a moment, as if she were recalling a happier time.

"I think Manuel and I fell in love at the very first meeting," she continued. "Afterward, we went for a soda and talked for a long, long time. That day we told each other everything about our lives."

Dolores paused before continuing. "As a reporter, you must know that the kind of life Manuel led was very different from mine. His parents were both born here, his father is a state senator, and his mother is a lawyer. My parents brought my brother and me to the United States from Mexico when we were little children. My father found work as a roofer, and Mama worked part-time as a waitress. Our father didn't speak any English, but Mama spoke it very well, so my brother and I, we picked up a lot from her. When my brother and I started school here, we had bilingual classes, and by the time we finished grade school, we were both speaking English as well as Mama. And now that I'm in high school . . ." She gave a wistful smile. "Manuel said he never would have guessed I wasn't born in the United States."

Liz nodded. "You speak extremely well." With a laugh, she added, "Better than some who've lived here all their lives."

The thought crossed her mind that Dolores and her family might be illegal immigrants. Like other New Yorkers, she was aware that, for a while, the city had become a mecca for undocumented aliens. But if Dolores and her brother were brought here as children, their parents must have been in the States for ten years or more. She told herself that this shouldn't concern her. She only wanted to find out more about Manuel.

"My father never spoke or understood more than a few

words of English," Dolores went on. Liz detected a note of resentment in her voice. "In his line of work there were many others like him, and also in the *barrio* where we lived. He might as well have been living in Mexico. He never even tried to learn the language. But Mama's speech was so good, she was able to go to night school and take some business courses. Lucky she did. My father died suddenly of a heart attack, and her part-time waitress work didn't pay enough for us to live on. Speaking good English and having typing and bookkeeping skills got her the job she still has, in the offices of a catering company. She makes enough for us to get by."

A slight frown crossed her face. "But my brother wanted to live in a bigger apartment in a better neighborhood," she said. "He told Mama that when he got old enough, he'd quit school and get a job. But Mama said if we were careful, we could live on what she made, and Ramon and I should stay in school and get our high-school diplomas, maybe even get student loans and go to college. All this I told Manuel the first day we met."

She paused, frowning again. "I told him how sad Mama was when Ramon dropped out of high school and joined the Zumas. He got good grades and could have gone to college, but he told us he was tired of being poor."

She paused before adding, "But he's making plenty of money now, and he has his own apartment. He's been very good to Mama and me. One thing he did was get us out of the *barrio* into a much nicer place to live."

Liz wanted to ask what sort of job Ramon had but didn't want to appear overly inquisitive. She wondered if he'd led his mother and sister to believe he had a well-paying job when actually he was dealing drugs. She told herself it was none of her concern. She only wanted to get more information on Manuel.

"When you first met Manuel, he wasn't a Serps member, was he?" she asked.

"Oh, no. Back then I don't believe he'd even thought of

joining a gang. I remember he talked a lot about his grandmother that first day. I could tell there was a special bond between them. It took a whole lot of those after-school meetings before he told me about his troubles in school and about his older brother, Julian, the model son who could do no wrong. Straight A's all through school, and now on the Dean's list at Princeton."

Liz got the picture. "Sounds like Manuel felt as if he couldn't measure up to his brother," she said.

Dolores nodded. "He told me his parents were always comparing him to Julian, and he knew he could never even come close to being the kind of son Julian was." Her face saddened. "I'll never forget the day he told me he'd joined *Las Serpientes* and was dropping out of school. I felt awful, but the worst part of it was, Manuel and Ramon being in gangs that hate each other."

She reached across the table and grasped Liz's hand. "Please, when you write your story, try to explain why Manuel joined a gang like *Las Serpientes.* With them being for Puerto Rican independence, and his father being a state senator opposed to it, Manuel figured the gang would admire him for standing up to his father, and he'd get the respect he never got at home."

If she were ever going to tell Dolores she wasn't a reporter, now would be the time, Liz thought. She thrust away the thought, asking, "Did he get the respect?"

Dolores nodded. "Yes—until the Serps found out about *me.* He knew they'd disapprove, and I knew my brother would disapprove too, so we kept it a secret. I didn't even tell Mama. We used to meet in Riverside Park or in the home of my best friend, a classmate at school."

"How did the Serps find out about you and Manuel?"

Dolores opened her purse and brought out a silver pin shaped like a serpent. "The uncle of one of the gang members is a silversmith who makes these for them," she replied. "Manuel gave this to me at Christmastime. I never wore it in plain sight, and when I wasn't wearing it, I kept it hidden, but one night when Ramon came to eat with Mama and me, I was careless and forgot to hide it. Ramon saw it."

"I guess he was angry."

"Yes. After I refused to tell him the name of the Serp who'd given it to me, he said he was going to the Serps' leader. I begged him not to. I told Mama everything, and she also begged Ramon to let it go. She said Manuel and I were both so young, it wouldn't last. But Ramon wouldn't listen."

"So, he confronted the Serps leader?"

"Yes. For once they were both on the same side. The Serps leader wanted to know who'd given me the pin, even more than Ramon did. The silversmith kept a record of who'd ordered the pins. That's how they found out it was Manuel who'd given me mine. He was ordered to break off with me."

"But you and Manuel kept on seeing each other?" '

Dolores nodded. "We had to sneak around even more than we had before. It was scary, but my best friend continued to help us meet."

Scary was an understatement, Liz thought. She'd heard enough about Manhattan's street gangs to know that members who disobeyed orders risked being marked for execution. Dolores and Manuel had taken a terrible chance—a chance that might have led to the brutal killing of Manuel. Images flashed into her mind of the mean-looking, scar-chinned Serp she'd seen in the church. He had the look of a cold-blooded killer.

She hesitated before asking a question she knew would be painful to Dolores. "When was the last time you saw Manuel?"

The look in Dolores' eyes made her wish she hadn't asked. But after a moment the barely audible reply came. "It was the night he was killed."

It didn't take Liz long to decide that the Serps had found out that Manuel was still seeing Dolores. Hoping for more details, she held back comments or questions. Her patience was rewarded a few moments later, when Dolores began to talk—her words pouring out, along with her tears.

"I was waiting for Manuel at my friend's place. It was his

birthday, and we'd planned a celebration with a cake and all. When he got there, he seemed very upset. For a while he wouldn't say why, but I kept asking him what was wrong, and at last he told me. He said his grandmother had knitted him a beautiful sweater for his birthday, but the minute he saw it, all he could think of was that the sweater would make him look like a college boy. It was something his brother Julian would wear. He said that made him mad, and he threw the sweater down and yelled at his grandmother, telling her it would make him look like a gringo nerd and he wouldn't be caught dead wearing it."

Over and over Liz had pictured the ugly scene in the Ruiz dining room. Now she found herself seeing it again, through different eyes. When Manuel stormed out of the Ruiz house, he'd gone directly to the home of Dolores' friend. Liz felt sure that Ike was not aware of Manuel's romance with Dolores, or where he'd gone on that fateful night. She'd have plenty to tell him tonight.

But something didn't make sense. How could Manuel, on his way home from his meeting with Dolores, have been found dead wearing the Argyle sweater? He'd left it behind when he made his angry exit from the house.

Dolores dabbed at her eyes with a tissue and continued. "Manuel told me he knew he'd hurt his beloved *abuela,* and he felt terrible and didn't know what to do. I told him he must return to his house and tell his grandmother he was sorry. I said he must put the sweater on and tell her he loved it. This, he agreed to do. He left, saying he'd be back soon. When he returned, he was wearing a beautiful, hand-knit sweater under his Serps jacket."

So that's how Manuel happened to be wearing the sweater when his body was found! Ike had ruled out the idea of Manuel's returning to the house that night. This information might turn his investigation upside down.

"Manuel said everyone had gone to bed by the time he got back to his house," Dolores went on. "The sweater was still in the dining room. He took off his Serps jacket and put the sweater on and went to his grandmother's bedroom. She was sound asleep. He didn't want to disturb her, so he left her a note telling her he was sorry for what he'd said. He told her he came back for the sweater and was wearing it now. He said he loved her and the sweater too, and tomorrow she'd see how nice it looked on him. He put the note in her knitting basket, where she'd find it first thing in the morning. He knew she always awakened very early and liked to do some knitting before breakfast."

But Liz remembered something Ike had told her. Broken-hearted after the scene at Manuel's birthday dinner, his grandmother had sworn she'd never knit anything again. Except for the interval when the needles had been taken for testing in the police lab, needles and yarn had lain, untouched, on a table near her window. She would not have opened her knitting basket; thus, she would not have found the note.

Liz felt a twinge of excitement. Ike and Lou would have had no reason to search the knitting basket for a potential murder weapon when they'd found the knitting needles out on the table, along with the yarn. *Manuel's note must still be in the basket, unread.* If only she could give Ike all this new information right now!

She pictured Manuel leaving his grandmother's bedroom wearing Argyle-patterned cashmere under serpent-logo polyester, stealing away from the house and his sleeping family members, returning to the house where Dolores was waiting. The Serps could have tailed him there and decided to kill him later, when he was on his way home.

But suppose a family member woke up when Manuel returned to the house—someone consumed with rage about Manuel's cruelty to his grandmother. Whoever it was could have followed him to the house of Dolores' friend, then lurked in that dark alley, ready to attack him while he was going home.

Engrossed in these thoughts, she barely heard Dolores' voice, trembling with sadness. "Manuel was so happy when he left to go home that night. He said he could hardly wait to go to his grandmother's bedroom the next morning, wearing the sweater. He was smiling when we kissed good night." Her voice broke. "I never saw him again."

Along with strong empathetic feelings, Liz felt qualms of self-reproach. Although she'd obtained a wealth of information to pass on to Ike, using Dolores to get it now struck her as shameful deception. For a moment she considered letting Dolores know she wasn't a reporter and telling her the whole truth.

But wouldn't this add to Dolores' pain and sorrow?

Before she could decide, Dolores spoke again. "Thank you for letting me tell you all this." With a glance at her watch, she added, "I should be leaving."

"Me too," Liz replied, feeling half regretful, half thankful, and thinking that Dolores would wonder why no article about Manuel ever appeared in any of the New York newspapers.

On their way out of the café, Dolores asked, "Are you taking the subway?"

Liz nodded. "Yes—downtown."

"I'm going uptown, but we can walk to the station together," Dolores said. "Maybe you'll think of something else you want to ask me for your article."

That was like throwing fresh fuel onto the embers of Liz's guilt, and the feelings flared again. She could no longer endure them. She had to come clean with Dolores.

On the sidewalk outside the café, she drew a deep breath and began. "Dolores, there's something I must tell you. . . ."

A gasp from Dolores cut her off. Liz turned and saw three burly young men jumping out of a shabby old car parked at the curb. Their black jackets, their orange and green bandanas, and the Puerto Rican flag flying from the car's antenna added up to a frightening fact. She and Dolores were in big trouble.

Chapter Fourteen

There was no time to run back into the café. The three Serps were upon them in seconds, and within those seconds, thoughts raced through Liz's mind. Dolores had been spotted in the church, after all. The forbidden girlfriend and the bogus reporter had been followed. Gang members didn't know that the woman they'd seen among the reporters was faking it. Did they believe Manuel had told Dolores some gang secrets, and she'd spilled the secrets to a reporter?

With mounting fear, she saw one of the Serps grab Dolores. Now she found herself staring into a pair of dark, mean-looking eyes, and she recognized the scarred chin of the Serp she'd seen leaving the church. As she felt his rough grip on her arm, her first instinct was to scream, but his hand had already closed over her mouth. She tried to knee him—a self-defense move Pop had taught her—but she was so weakened by fear, it didn't come off one hundred percent. Though his grip lessened for a moment, he didn't let go of her. His renewed hold, brutally tight, told her he felt more anger than pain.

Passersby could not help but notice, Liz thought. Surely some male pedestrian would intervene, or someone would call 911.

She should have known better. New Yorkers were notorious for carrying "mind your own business" to the nth degree. *Why interfere in a squabble among young men and their girlfriends?* Besides, those orange and green bandanas identified the youths as gang members. People didn't want to get mixed up with them.

Now Scarred Chin called to Dolores, "Do as we say, *muchacha,* and nobody gets hurt. We know you got the pin on you, or they wouldn't let you into the church. Give it up—now."

"Yeah, let's have it, or we'll have to get rough," Dolores' assailant, a big, beefy guy, said. The third Serp, standing by, leered at her.

At that moment Liz saw a sleek, late-model car, a Mercedes, double-parking near the Serps' shabby old heap. She noticed a crude painting of a crown on the back. Putting two and two together, she figured it was the crown of the Aztec ruler, Montezuma. The car must belong to a member of the Zuma gang. Her heart sank. Were she and Dolores about to get mixed up in a gang fight?

Three men got out of the car. One advanced ahead of the others and shouted a volley of Spanish words, followed by an order in English.

"Just take your hands off my sister, and there won't be any trouble."

His sister! Liz never dreamed she'd want to lay eyes on Dolores' drug-dealing brother, much less be glad to see him, but, as he approached, followed by two other young men, she felt deeply thankful.

She appraised Ramon Otero with some surprise. Tall, muscular, well-barbered, clean-shaven, and dressed in neat brown slacks and a brown Windbreaker, he did not fit the stereotype of a gang member. His companions too looked more like ordinary high school or college students than members of a street gang. All three bore only one sign of a gang connection—their purple and yellow bead necklaces. An amusing thought struck her. It was as if the Zumas were trying to convey the image of gentlemen gang members.

Dolores' Serp assailant removed one hand from across her mouth and the other from her arm and responded in English. "Okay, Otero, you say you know you're off your turf, but you're not looking for trouble. You say let go of your sister, and there won't be none. We don't want no trouble, neither. We're just taking our pin back. She got no right to it."

Sobbing, Dolores broke away and ran into her brother's arms. "Please, Ramon, don't let them take my pin."

Liz's heart went out to her. The silver serpent pin was all Dolores had left of her romance with Manuel.

All Ramon's attention was on Dolores, as if he hadn't noticed Liz in Scarred Chin's clutches, but Scarred Chin let go of her, anyway. Her first thought was to go for the cell phone in her purse and punch in 911. Common sense stopped her. Her phone would be the seized the instant she brought it out. Better to keep it out of sight. Maybe she'd get a chance to use it later.

Instead, she took a step toward Ramon, saying, "I can tell you love your sister, and I'm sure you can understand what the pin means to her. Can't you find it in your heart to let her keep it?"

Ramon's dark eyes appraised her. "Who are you?" he asked.

"She's a reporter," Scarred Chin snarled. He gestured toward the café. "She and your sister, they been in there. You can bet she got your sister talking. You should be worried about that, Otero."

"I'm not a reporter," Liz said. She turned to Dolores. "I wanted to tell you. . . ."

Dolores, clinging to her brother, nodded. "That's true, Ramon. I remember that just before we were grabbed, she said she had something to tell me."

"If she's no reporter, why was she with the other reporters in the church?" Scarred Chin asked. "Search her bag, Otero. It's ten to one you'll find ID to prove I'm right."

"Go ahead and search my bag. You won't find anything that identifies me as a reporter," Liz replied. "I was attending the funeral service with a friend who works for one of the newspapers."

With narrowed eyes, Ramon Otero cast her a long, studying look. She felt sure he was going to say he didn't believe her. Instead, to her surprise, he turned to the Serps, saying, "If she's a reporter, she wouldn't be so willing to have her bag searched. I'll find out later what she is. Right now I want to settle the matter of the pin my sister has. Just because it's a Serps pin doesn't mean you have a right to take it. It was given to her as a gift. That makes it her property."

Dolores responded in a voice choked with grateful tears. "Oh, *gracias,* Ramon! Thank you, thank you!"

Pleased and surprised as Liz was, as well, she felt a stab of apprehension. Ramon and his two gang brothers were in Serps territory, and now Ramon was refusing to give up a pin the Serps considered theirs. This challenge could turn a mild confrontation into a scene of violence. But at that moment a wail of police sirens sounded. Someone had put in a call, after all, she thought, with a feeling of relief.

Like rats deserting a sinking ship, the three Serps scattered. Their old car with the Puerto Rican flag whipping from its antenna rattled away just as two NYPD vehicles screeched onto the scene. Liz expected one of them to follow in pursuit. Instead, both cars stopped, and four officers got out. They must have sized up the situation and decided a high-speed chase wasn't warranted, she thought.

Unlike the scurrying Serps, Ramon and his cohorts made no move to jump into the Mercedes and take off. Instead, Ramon, with Dolores still clinging to his arm, strode toward the approaching cops. The others lingered behind.

Liz felt more curious than surprised. She'd already pegged the Zumas as somewhat different from the typical Manhattan street gang, especially Ramon.

Her estimation was reinforced when Ramon greeted the cops with an earnest smile. "Good thing you showed up, Officers." As he spoke, he drew Dolores closer to him and cast her a look of unmistakable affection.

Liz felt sure that his words and actions were meant to convey a distinct impression. Police had arrived just in time to avert a gang fight involving a young woman with ties to the Zumas. The scrambling departure of the Serps indicated guilt.

Meanwhile, police presence at the scene had drawn the attention of passersby. Several people stopped to see what was going on.

Here was her opportunity to get out of the predicament, Liz thought. She had two choices. A few words to the officers would do it, or, now that the cops' arrival had diverted everyone's attention, she could slip away unnoticed. Either way, she'd be home free.

But she wasn't sure if Ike's precinct covered this area. If it did, there was a good chance Ike would hear she was involved in an incident with the Serps before she got a chance to tell him herself. Although she hadn't exactly broken her promise to steer clear of the Serps, she'd come close. Instead of presenting herself to the cops, maybe she should just quietly leave the scene before they noticed her.

While trying to decide which course to take, she noticed the officers scrutinizing Dolores. "This your girlfriend?" one of them asked Ramon.

Gently, Ramon smoothed a stray lock of hair away from Dolores' brow. "She's my kid sister," he replied.

The reply, with its accompanying gesture, obviously made a favorable impression on the cops. Their flinty facial expressions softened, as if they were thinking that maybe this confrontation wasn't hormone-driven rivalry between two hostile Latino gangs over some female. This was a brother defending his sister.

But were the cops also thinking that the Zumas might use this incident as a reason to launch a major battle in their ongoing war with the Serps? Liz wondered.

Ramon's next statement answered her question. "I assure you, as far as I'm concerned, there'll be no more trouble about this," he told the officers. "I'm willing to call it a misunderstanding."

Liz had to admire his strategy. He'd clearly established the Serps as the guilty ones in the incident and himself as a reasonable man who wanted only to protect his sister.

Suddenly she realized that her interest in the encounter between Ramon Otero and the officers had diverted her from deciding whether to stay or go. Just as she made up her mind to slip away, she knew it was too late. With no reason to linger at the scene, the cops started returning to their vehicles, the curious crowd began to disperse, and Ramon turned his full attention to her.

With one arm still around Dolores, he said, "Señorita, I need to know if you are a reporter or not."

His manner was almost apologetic, Liz thought, digging into her bag for her wallet. Again she had to admire his technique. He was a smooth guy with a gift for coming across as sincere. He'd make a good con man. Maybe that came in handy with drug dealing.

"Here's my work ID," she said, handing it to him.

He looked at it. "The city morgue!" he exclaimed, sounding surprised and curious. Liz could tell he was picturing her attending to corpses.

Accustomed to that reaction, she explained that she was on the medical examiner's clerical staff. "Nothing to do with the bodies."

With a final glance at the ID, he gave it back to her. "Okay, I'm satisfied you're not a reporter," he replied. "But I'd like to know what you and my sister were talking about in the café."

Liz cast a questioning glance at Dolores. After a moment's hesitation, Dolores spoke up. "Ramon, I'll tell you myself what we were talking about. I thought she was a reporter wanting to write a story about Manuel. I followed her out of the church and told her I wanted to talk with her. I wanted her to know as much as possible about Manuel, so she would understand, and she would write a true story. In the café, I told her everything I knew about—" Her voice broke as she spoke the final words of her explanation. ". . . about the man I loved and will always love."

An expression close to anger crossed Ramon's face. It was gone in an instant, replaced by a smile and an agreeable, "All right. I guess that wraps it up."

He glanced at his watch. Liz noticed it was a Rolex. "Dolores, I have business uptown near my place," he said. "I'll drop you off on my way there, but I'll come back later and stay the night with you and Mama."

Turning to Liz, he said, "Señorita, I'll be glad to drive you home."

"Thanks, but you're going uptown—it will be out of your way," she replied.

"I don't mind a detour," he said. "Whereabouts do you live?"

With Dolores included in the ride, Liz had no misgivings about accepting his offer of a lift home. Besides, the confrontation with the Serps had given her an idea. She could question Ramon Otero during the ride and get some information about Scarred Chin. Maybe she'd learn something more to pass on to Ike.

But the last thing she needed was to have a drug-dealing gang member knowing where she lived. She didn't want to offend Ramon by appearing reluctant to give her address. Although she was close to getting out of this predicament, she sensed that the wrong choice of words could change everything. She could end up in worse trouble than before. She did some quick thinking and came up with the solution.

"Oh, thanks. I live in the Gramercy Park area," she replied. "But I need to buy food for dinner tonight. Could you drop me off at a grocery a few blocks from my place?"

It was a lie, of course. When she'd passed the Moscarettis' door on her way out that morning, Rosa had hailed her, saying she was going to make eggplant parmegiana that night.

"I'm making enough for you and Ike," she'd said. "Stop by when you get home and pick it up."

Apparently the lie was convincing. "Sure," Ramon said, turning toward the Mercedes. "Let's go."

After seating Dolores in the front, Ramon got behind the

wheel with a distinct air of ownership. The Mercedes was his, Liz thought, wedged between the two other Zumas in back. Unless Ramon had a lucrative job, the Mercedes, the Rolex, and the apartment where he lived were being financed with drug money. And drug money might also be helping pay rent on the nicer place he'd found for Dolores and their mother.

When the car started off, she contemplated how to broach the subject of Scarred Chin to Ramon. If she said he seemed very mean, that might get Ramon talking. Maybe he'd tell her enough for her to know whether Scarred Chin was capable of a brutal murder. But before she could begin, she heard Ramon's voice, scolding Dolores, in English. Apparently Spanish was a secondary language for them.

"How many times did I tell you not to go to that funeral? How many times did I warn you, you'd get into trouble? Lucky I figured you wouldn't listen to me."

And lucky the Serps had a Puerto Rican flag flying from their antenna, Liz thought. That had made it easy for Ramon to spot their car after the funeral service, when he drove around the area near the church in search of his sister. She had only to recall Scarred Chin's mean eyes to feel grateful Ramon had found them.

She barely heard Dolores' voice. "I had to go to the funeral, Ramon. If you were in love, you'd understand."

Ramon's voice sounded angry, and what he said was cruel. "Love! What do you know about it? You think that Puerto Rican senator's son loved you because he gave you the Serps pin? He was only playing with you—and playing at being a Serp too. It wouldn't have been long before he dumped you and the gang and gone back to being a rich American boy with no more use for a Mexican girl."

When Dolores made no reply, Liz suspected that the girl was in tears. Didn't Ramon realize his words would break his sister's heart?

Why had he allowed Dolores to keep the Serps' pin? It had nothing to do with brotherly love, she decided. It was a power play, she thought—a Zuma getting the better of enemy gang members on their own territory. Ramon had taken a big risk. He was lucky the cops had showed up before the Serps could phone their members for backup.

A sudden, strong suspicion struck her. *Before Ramon got out of his Mercedes, had he put in the call to the police himself?*

At that moment, the Zumas in the backseat started speaking to each other in Spanish. Did they want to keep her from understanding their talk?

She recognized a few words from her two years of high school Spanish. They'd said *hermana*—that meant *sister*, and *linda*—that meant *pretty*. They were saying that Ramon's sister was pretty. No big secret there. Most likely they were conversing in Spanish because they spoke little or no English, she decided.

Ramon must have overheard their remarks. She saw him glance into the rearview mirror at them. He made a brief comment in rapid Spanish. She couldn't pick up what he said, but her fleeting glimpse of his face in the mirror and the tone of his voice suggested he was not pleased with their comments about Dolores. Ramon was overprotective of his sister, Liz thought. He didn't like his gang brothers commenting on her obvious charms.

With that insight, another thought settled into her mind. If Ramon got hot under the collar whenever he heard men discussing his sister, he must have really flared up when he found out that a man from an enemy gang had captured Dolores' heart. She recalled the flash of anger she'd seen on his face when Dolores stated that she'd always love Manuel.

But if she were going to get any information about Scarred Chin, she'd better not delay. "Ramon," she said, "I'm curious about that Serp who had a hold on me before you came to the rescue. He seemed so mean."

Ramon looked at her in the rearview mirror and nodded. "He's a mean one, all right, but he's not much worse than any of those other Puerto Ricans."

She wanted to ask more questions, but she sensed that his

remark had added to the heartache Dolores was already feeling. Answers to further questions might have the same result.

When Ramon braked the Mercedes near the grocery store, Liz thanked him and gave Dolores a gentle pat on the shoulder as she got out.

While she watched the car blend into traffic, her mind teemed with speculation. She'd spent the past six days trying to figure out who had murdered Manuel Ruiz. Since day one, she'd suspected various members of the Ruiz family but couldn't figure out how Manuel had been found wearing the sweater when he'd left the house without it. Now that she knew he'd returned to the house, it looked as if a family member might have seen him leave his grandmother's bedroom and followed him back to where Dolores was waiting.

But she must not lose sight of the possibility that the Serps had found out where Manuel and Dolores were holding their forbidden meetings and that Manuel's murder had been gang-ordered. She pictured the Serp with the mean eyes and the scarred chin as the designated killer.

Too bad she hadn't been able to get much about him from Ramon. She'd hoped to pick up some important information for Ike. The more she had to tell Ike, the less disapproving he'd be when she confessed what she'd gotten herself into today. But even without information about Scarred Chin, how could Ike be anything but pleased with what she'd found out from Dolores?

While she was walking the few blocks home, reflecting, a sudden, startling thought struck her. With lightning speed, new suspicions crowded her mind, and a new face loomed in the lineup of possible killers.

Ramon! Could his extreme protectiveness of his sister have led him to murder Manuel?

Chapter Fifteen

When Ike stepped into Liz's apartment that evening, all smiles, Liz took that as a good sign. It had to mean he hadn't gotten wind of the police report about a gang confrontation near the church where Manuel's funeral was held. Knowing she'd been in the vicinity, and mindful of her ability to get into predicaments, he might not look so jolly. She'd tell him about it after they'd eaten.

He gave her a hug and a kiss. "Something smells great," he said with a glance toward the kitchen area.

"Thanks to Rosa," Liz replied. "Eggplant parmegiana. I'm heating it in the micro. She gave us some Italian bread too, and I made a salad. I'll have everything on the table in a couple of minutes."

He nodded. "Good. I'll pour the wine."

Seated at the table, they raised their goblets. "Here's to two weeks from Saturday," Ike said with a big smile.

Two weeks from Saturday—their wedding day!

Over the rim of her glass, she returned the smile. "Oh, *yes!* To our big day."

How quickly the time had passed since last summer, when they'd set the date for their wedding, she thought, and especially since they went to get their marriage license several weeks ago. Before they knew it, the big day would be here.

She thought about adding to her toast by saying, "And to the quick solution of Manuel Ruiz's murder," but she decided against it. Ike might take that as a hint for him to share more information with her. She didn't want him to feel compelled to tell her something he wasn't ready to divulge.

That thought had barely crossed her mind when Ike raised his glass again, saying, "And here's to wrapping up the Ruiz case."

She looked at him in surprise. Had some new evidence brought him closer to making an arrest? If so, this would be the first case they'd worked on together for which she hadn't dug up some helpful information. She felt a pang of regret. What Dolores had provided, and the speculation about Ramon, suddenly seemed useless.

But his next remark cheered her. "Not that it's anywhere near wrapped up, but let's drink to it, anyway, and then you can tell me if you got any hot clues at the funeral."

He was teasing her, she thought as they touched glasses. She felt tempted to tell him, right then, about her talk with Dolores Otero, the incident with the Serps and Zumas, and her suspicions about Ramon, but she decided the time was not right. He'd be far from pleased when she described her encounter with the gang members. Better to stick to her original intention and hold off telling him until he'd eaten. With Rosa's good food under his belt, he might take her latest scrape with better humor.

"Sorry, I didn't pick up on anything in the church," she replied. "How about you?"

"Just something that struck me as strange," Ike said. "From where I was sitting, I had a good view of Uncle Carlos and his mother. The old lady was all broken up, and during the service I noticed he devoted all his attention to her."

Liz nodded. "I saw the grandmother weeping almost uncontrollably when they followed the casket out of the church, and he was trying to console her."

"That's understandable," Ike said, "But here's what I found strange. I watched him very carefully throughout the service, and I didn't see him look toward the casket even once."

Liz stared at him, trying to figure out the full meaning of his statement. Was he implying that Uncle Carlos Ruiz could not bear to look at the casket containing the body of the young nephew he, himself, had slain?

"Do you think Carlos was so enraged at Manuel for hurting the grandmother that he could have done such a horrible thing to his own nephew?" she asked.

"I've been giving that some thought right from the start," Ike replied. "He has an unusually strong devotion to his mother, and he was probably very angry at Manuel for hurting her. When I noticed he never looked at the casket during the service, it reinforced my suspicions. But in my experience, when a person kills someone in anger, he's generally driven by something more powerful than devotion."

Liz thought for a moment. "Like jealousy?"

"Yeah. I've covered enough homicide cases to know that extreme jealousy can drive a person out of control, but I've never seen anyone turn into a killer because of something like devotion to a third person, even a family member."

Liz thought immediately of Ramon's extreme protectiveness of Dolores. Wouldn't that be on the same emotional level as family devotion and thus unlikely to trigger a homicidal rage? She needed to discuss the matter with Ike. The time had come for her to let him know what had happened after Manuel's funeral, starting with finding out that Manuel had returned to the house for the sweater and ending with her suspicions about Ramon Otero.

She drew a deep breath. "I have something to tell you."

He cast her a penetrating look. "I get the feeling I'm not going to like it. What have you been up to now?"

She began by telling him about noticing Dolores in the church and Sam's saying she was probably Manuel's forbidden girlfriend. "She followed me when I left the church. She thought I was a reporter, and—"

Frowning, Ike broke in. "And you didn't let her know you're not?"

Liz shook her head. "She wanted to tell me all about Manuel so I could write a truthful story about him. I thought it would be a chance for me to pick up something that would help you on the case."

"I guess I can't berate you for that," Ike said. "Did you find out anything?"

"Yes. The girl told me a few things you and Lou might not know."

She related what Dolores had told her about the secret romance with Manuel and about his going home to put the sweater on and make peace with his grandmother and about his leaving his *abuela* a note in her knitting basket before returning to his other birthday party. She held off mentioning anything about Ramon Otero or the incident between the Serps and the Zumas. She wanted to give Ike the helpful information first. Maybe he'd be so pleased with it, he wouldn't blow his stack when she told him the rest.

Early in her dissertation, Ike started smiling, and by the time she finished, he'd broken into a broad grin. He reached across the table and clasped her hand.

"This is great stuff, Redlocks. You're right, we hadn't found out yet that Manuel had a secret girlfriend. I'd been thinking all along that Manuel might have returned to the house to apologize to his grandmother and put the sweater on, but every time I gave it some serious consideration, I found myself up against a negative. If he *did* come back, his grandmother would have been in a different frame of mind the next morning."

He paused to give her hand a gentle squeeze. "What Manuel's girlfriend told you sheds new light on the case. Lou and I will pay a visit to the Ruiz household first thing tomorrow and look for that note in the knitting basket."

"After you told me that Carlos Ruiz avoided looking at his nephew's casket, I thought what I was going to tell you would make him your number-one suspect," Liz said. "I thought you'd decide that he saw Manuel come out of the grandmother's bedroom and followed him out of the house and waited for him in that dark alley. But then you said that something like devotion to a third person wouldn't trigger a homicidal rage."

"Yeah, I've seen jealousy involving a spouse or a lover do that, but never devotion like Carlos Ruiz has for his mother."

"So you don't think Uncle Carlos is the killer?"

"I'm not eliminating anybody yet." He gave her hand a gentle pat. "But you certainly solved the puzzle we've been scratching our heads over. Nice work, Redlocks."

Now that she had him feeling grateful, this would be the ideal time to let him know what else had happened, she decided. "There's more," she said.

"More?" He looked surprised and a bit wary.

"Yes . . ." She jumped right into it and left nothing out.

He listened without interruption. Only a slight tightening of his mouth indicated that he didn't like what he was hearing.

She tried to end up on a positive note. "I wasn't in any real danger, and we now have another possible suspect—the Serp with the scarred chin. We might even have two suspects, if you want to include Dolores' protective Zuma brother."

"Whether or not you were in danger is debatable," Ike replied. "If the cops hadn't shown up, God knows what could have happened." He managed a weak smile. "But you're right about the Serp with the scarred chin. He sounds like a possible suspect."

"How about the overly protective Zuma brother?" she asked.

"I can see where he'd be angry about his sister dating a Serp and do his best to break them up, but I can't picture him flying into a homicidal rage over it. In my experience, brotherly affection and protective instincts don't ignite the urge to kill the way jealousy of a spouse or a lover can."

Liz thought of the many possible suspects in the case. "It's a good thing Dolores is Ramon's sister," she said. "You have more than enough people to investigate."

He nodded, giving her hand another pat. "We'll start

working with detectives on gang detail and find out the name of the Serp with the scarred chin. With that noticeable a disfigurement, it shouldn't be difficult to identify him. A background check will tell us if he's ever been arrested for assault, attempted homicide, or other violent behavior."

Liz felt pleased that his reaction to her latest scrape had turned out better than she'd expected. "So, all's well that ends well," she said.

He shook his head. "It's not as simple as that. The dispute over the Serps pin could mean more trouble between the two gangs, and trouble for Manuel's girlfriend too. If the Serps don't already know where she lives, they'll make it their business to find out. Tonight they might send some members to get the pin away from her."

Liz remembered Ramon's remark about spending the night with Dolores and their mother. She mentioned that to Ike.

"Looks like he's on top of the situation," Ike said. He paused, looking puzzled. "But, there's something I can't figure out. With the bad blood between the Zumas and the Serps, why would Ramon let his sister keep the pin?"

"I wondered about that too," Liz said. "He stood right there on Serps turf, bold as brass, and told them the pin was given to Dolores as a gift and that that made it her property. It was almost as if he wanted the Serps to start something. Do you think he figures a big gang battle might divert police surveillance from the Zumas' drug trafficking?"

Ike laughed. "You might be on to something there, Redlocks."

Despite the laugh, she got the feeling her question had started a new train of thought in Ike's mind. She held back her impatience. He'd let her in on it when he was ready.

They finished eating, then, as usual, took coffee to the sofa and turned on the TV.

Snuggling into Ike's arms, Liz said, "I realize, on a scale from one to ten, what happened today between the two gangs wouldn't rate very high in the 'hot news' category, but do you think there might be some TV coverage?"

"Could be," he replied. "Reporters check the police blotters. If they can't find enough important or sensational stuff, they go with what's there."

On the TV screen, a handsome black man was delivering the national news. A perky, long-haired blond followed him, giving the national and local weather report. After that, another young woman, equally perky but with long dark hair, came on with the local news.

They listened to her report on the robbery of a lower Broadway pizza parlor and watched taped coverage of a big traffic pileup on Fifth Avenue due to a vehicular accident. Also reported was an accident at a construction site on the Upper East Side, where three workers had been injured. Then came a report about Manuel Ruiz's funeral and a shot of the casket being borne out of the church.

Just as Liz was thinking there'd be no coverage of the gang confrontation, it came on.

"Police averted a possible battle between members of two street gangs in midtown Manhattan this afternoon. . . ."

With no cameras at the scene, the coverage, like the incident itself, was brief. A commercial break followed.

"Looks like that's it for the news," Ike said. "What's on the old-movie channel tonight?"

"Let's see," Liz replied, clicking the remote. "I usually know what's on, but today I didn't have time to look it up."

"Yeah, you were too busy trying to get into trouble," Ike blurted. In the next instant, he gave her a hug. "Forget I said that. I know you never deliberately set out to get yourself into dangerous situations."

She gave a rueful sigh. "I didn't think there'd be anything risky about having coffee with Manuel's girlfriend."

She should have known he'd remind her of past predicaments she'd gotten herself into.

"Just like you didn't think there'd be anything risky about spending a weekend posing as a chambermaid in the house where Countess Zanardi was murdered," Ike said, "or snooping around the school where the teacher was strangled and thrown off the gym balcony, or . . ." He paused, firming his arms around her. "I worry about you, Liz. I don't know what I'd do if I didn't have you in my life."

She kissed his cheek and looked into his eyes. "You'll always have me in your life. I promise I'll try to be more careful."

Sudden musical fanfare from the TV drew their attention. A movie was coming on.

"*Run Silent, Run Deep*!" Ike exclaimed. "Clark Gable."

Submarine warfare, Liz thought with an inner sigh. She would have preferred a Fred Astaire/Ginger Rogers musical, or a Cary Grant/Irene Dunne comedy, but Ike enjoyed World War II movies. She told herself she might as well get used to watching them.

"I'll get refills on our coffee," she said.

When the movie ended, she agreed with him that it was one of the best old black-and-white films they'd ever viewed.

"After we're married and settled into our apartment, I'd like to get one of those super-big-screen TVs," Ike said. "It will be like watching films in a movie theater."

"Meanwhile, we'll have to make do with my dinky little set," Liz replied.

"Yeah, and meanwhile I have to go back to my own place every night," he growled.

"Only for two more weeks," she said.

"Guess I can endure it," he replied with a grin. Rising from the sofa, he added, "As soon as we've done the dishes, I should be heading home."

He was going to work online on the case, Liz figured. Well, the more extra time he put in on it, the sooner the case would be solved.

"Don't worry about the dishes," she said.

He returned the smile. "Thanks. I want to get a head start on tomorrow. I have a ton of work lined up, starting with a visit to the Ruiz home for a look into the grandmother's sewing basket."

"And then a look into Scarred Chin's background?"

"Right." At the door he gave her a firm hug and a long kiss. "What you found out today is going to be a big help. Good night, Redlocks."

After she'd opened the sofa bed, Liz turned the TV to a news channel. Any coverage of the Manuel's murder would probably be old stuff, but she wanted to make sure. Flipping through news channels, she found nothing new except for some shots of the church after the funeral.

She didn't feel at all sleepy, so she turned back to the movie channel and caught the beginning of another World War II movie. John Wayne was in this one. She decided to watch it and told herself she should learn to enjoy war films as much as Ike did. If he bought one of those huge-screen TVs, he'd get a DVD player too, and he'd probably want to build a library of every World War II movie ever made.

Although it was late by the time the movie ended, and even though she knew anything about the Ruiz case would be a rehash, she couldn't resist turning on a news channel again. After watching a few minutes of coverage she'd seen several times before, she began to feel drowsy. She was about to turn the TV off and settle in for the night, when a bulletin came on.

"A young Latino man was found stabbed and evidently left for dead on an Upper West Side street tonight," the newscaster announced. "The victim was taken to a hospital, where he remains in critical condition. No further details are available at this time."

Chapter Sixteen

The bulletin's brevity and its abrupt termination left Liz unconcerned for a few moments. But echoes of the newscaster's words lingered in her mind. "*. . . a young Latino man.*" Suddenly she found herself confronted by a startling question. *Could the victim possibly be Ramon Otero?*

Wide awake now and hoping details would soon be forthcoming, she kept the TV on. Had Ike heard the bulletin? Not likely. He was probably working online. Although it was almost midnight, maybe he was still at it.

When, at quarter past twelve, there'd been no more coverage of the stabbing, she felt a strong need to discuss it with Ike. She decided to phone him. By now, chances were he had quit working.

He picked up on the first ring, sounding surprised. "You still awake, Liz? What's up?"

She told him about the bulletin, adding, "After what happened this afternoon, I couldn't help thinking the victim might be Ramon Otero."

Ike said he hadn't heard the bulletin. "I've been working and just called it quits a few minutes ago," he said. "But, yeah, after what happened this afternoon, it might be Otero. Sounds as if some of the Serps could have gone to Dolores' place to get the pin, not knowing her brother would be there. Maybe Ramon saw or heard them outside the apartment and went to investigate. What started out as an attempt to get the pin back might have turned into a retaliatory attack on Ramon. Did the bulletin mention the name of the hospital?"

"No, only that the victim's under police guard and in

critical condition. But if the victim was Ramon, would there be a connection to Manuel's murder? Do you think whoever stabbed him could also have killed Manuel?"

"I guess it's possible. The attack tonight happened outside our precinct, but we'll contact the other squad tomorrow and see what we can find out."

"Before you go to the Ruiz house to find the note in the sewing basket?"

"We'll look for the note first."

That answer brought another question into her mind. If Ike suspected that the Serps were responsible for both Manuel's murder and an attack on Ramon Otero, why wouldn't he want to look into that night's stabbing first?

She recalled his remarks concerning Uncle Carlos at Manuel's funeral. The man hadn't given the casket so much as a glance during the service. Did that mean Ike suspected Carlos Ruiz? She shook her head, remembering he'd also told her that he'd never come up against a killer who'd been motivated by familial devotion rather than, say, romantic jealousy.

"Tomorrow's going to be a full day for you," she said.

"Yeah. I doubt if there'll be any more news about this tonight. We should both get some sleep. I'll call you at work tomorrow, around four, and let you know when I can get away for dinner."

But, late as it was after they said good night, she couldn't get to sleep. If the stabbing victim were Ramon Otero, then Ike was right—a plan to get the Serps pin from Dolores could have turned into the attack on Ramon in retaliation for his bold actions earlier that day. In her mind's eye she saw Scarred Chin leading the attack and doing the actual stabbing.

She went over what Ramon had said to Dolores in the car. He planned to spend the night with her and their mother. Judging from the time the bulletin was broadcast, the attack must have taken place very late tonight. The Serps must have known where Dolores and her mother lived, and also that Ramon did not live with them. But when they got to the apartment, they would have noticed a Mercedes parked nearby.

The Aztec symbol painted on the rear would have left no doubt it was Ramon's car.

That's probably when the plan to get the pin from Dolores changed into a plan to punish Ramon for challenging Serps in their own territory, she thought. Now her imagination really took off. She pictured Scarred Chin and his cohorts gathered around the Mercedes, deliberately raising their voices loudly enough to be heard by nearby apartment residents. But of all those who might have looked out their windows to see what was going on in the street in the middle of the night, only Ramon would have taken action. His Mercedes would have been the only car with shadowy figures lurking around it. But when he rushed out to confront them, wouldn't he have suspected they were Serps? Maybe, as he fingered his knife, he was confident in his ability to deal with more than one of them. Evidently he had been greatly outnumbered.

She wanted to call Ike back to express those thoughts but decided against it. He'd be asleep by now. She'd have to wait until tomorrow night.

Meanwhile, her mind continued to churn with vivid speculation until she fell asleep at last.

Liz's first thought in the morning was yet another question. Had the stabbing victim made it through the night, or, like Manuel, had his life gushed away with the blood from his wounds?

She turned the TV on and listened while making coffee and getting ready to go to work. No follow-up to last night's bulletin was forthcoming. Again the questions plagued her. Was the stabbing victim Ramon Otero, and was he still alive?

Well, she'd soon have some answers, she thought, finishing her coffee. Dan would let her know if the body of a young Latino male stabbing victim had been brought into the morgue.

Chapter Seventeen

"Sorry, Lizzie, I don't have a report of a body answering that description," Dan said. He cast her a quizzical look. "You want to fill me in?"

"Sure," Liz replied. "I would have given you the details already, but I thought you might be busy, and . . ."

"I'm never too busy to hear about your sleuthing. Why are you interested in a body answering that description?"

"It's kind of a long story. . . ." Liz described her meeting with Dolores Otero after the funeral and the incident involving the Serps and Ramon.

"Luckily, Dolores' brother appeared on the scene with two other Zumas," she said. She hadn't yet mentioned the TV bulletin about the attack on the young man she presumed to be Ramon, when Dan broke in with a slight frown.

"That was a close call, Lizzie. Does Ike know about it?"

"Yes, and at first *he* wasn't happy about it, either."

" 'At first'? Did you come up with some information about the Ruiz case? Does Ike think this girl's brother had anything to do with it?"

"No, but he thinks the Serps might be involved, especially the one who had me in his clutches. He's going to look into his background. But you haven't heard everything yet." She told him about last night's news bulletin.

"So, you think the body you asked about might be this Ramon Otero?"

Liz nodded. "There's been nothing more on the news about the stabbing. I've been wondering if he made it through the night. But you don't have a report on a body that might be his, so I guess he's still in the hospital."

"How do you always mange to get involved in risky situations with shady characters?" Dan asked, half chiding, half joking.

She flashed him a semiregretful smile. "I don't intend to. Sometimes it just happens."

Turning to go, she said, "I'd better get to work. I came in early this morning to help make up for the time off you gave me to attend the funeral."

"Okay, Lizzie. And if the body of a young Hispanic male comes in, with or without ID, I'll let you know."

Did the stabbing victim have his wallet with ID on him when he was found, Liz asked herself on the way to her workstation, or, like Manuel's, had it been taken and thrown away by whoever stabbed him? The feeling persisted that the man in the hospital was Ramon Otero and that the attack was linked, somehow, to Manuel's murder.

The morning passed without any word from Dan, but when Liz turned her desk TV on before going out for lunch, she caught a news report on the hospitalized man she thought might be Dolores Otero's brother.

"A driver's license in a wallet found on last night's Upper West Side stabbing victim has identified him as Ramon Otero, known to be a member of the Montezumas, one of the city's Hispanic gangs," the newscaster stated. "Otero remains hospitalized, in critical condition."

Brief as it was, the news report answered some of the questions crowding Liz's mind. The victim was, indeed, Ramon, and he was still alive. Also, his wallet had not been taken. This made her wonder if whoever killed Manuel was the same person or persons who'd attacked Ramon.

But, assuming the Serps made the attack on Ramon . . . If, indeed, Ramon Otero was dealing drugs, they'd know about it, and they'd expect his wallet to be full of large-denomination bills. She couldn't imagine their passing up the chance to get their hands on it—especially Scarred Chin. He looked like the kind of person who'd even rob a grave. Most likely they'd seen or heard someone approaching, and a quick getaway had been necessary. No time to go through Ramon's pockets.

Sophie phoned during the afternoon. Before Liz could begin to tell her about the funeral, the incident with the gang members, and the attempt on Ramon's life, Sophie jumped right in with a question.

"How busy are you right now?"

From the tone of her voice, Liz knew she had something interesting to divulge. Her own news could wait.

"I can spare a few minutes," she replied.

"I guess you heard a gang member was found stabbed last night, and he's in a hospital in critical condition," Sophie said. "Well, we just got word that if this guy dies, there'll be a major gang battle between his gang, the Zumas, and a Puerto Rican gang, the Serps. If other gangs take sides, the west side will be like a war zone. The entire NYPD has been alerted, and the chief is trying to arrange a meeting with gang leaders to head it off, but if this Zuma doesn't make it, there's sure to be bloodshed."

"That's scary. Let's hope he makes it," Liz replied. Not only to avert an all-out gang war but for the sake of Dolores and her mother, she thought. She felt a rush of sympathy for them.

She knew she must tell Sophie about yesterday's happenings before Sophie had to ring off. Making it as brief as possible, she described it all, starting with her meeting Dolores after the funeral.

"That Zuma member in the hospital is Dolores' brother, Ramon Otero," she concluded.

"Wow," Sophie said. "I know you wouldn't keep this from Ike. How did he react?"

"He wasn't pleased, but he got over it. I haven't talked with him since the stabbed man was identified."

"Sounds to me like this guy was deliberately trying to stir up trouble with the other gang."

"That's exactly what I thought."

"Why would he want to do that?" Sophie asked. He should have known the other gang would come after him." Almost in the same breath, she said, "Oops, I gotta go. Maybe we'll get a chance to talk later."

Good question, Sophie, Liz thought, as she clicked off. Why would Ramon deliberately want to provoke the Serps?

Ike phoned at four o'clock. "Did you catch the news bulletin saying the stabbing victim has been identified as Ramon Otero?" he asked.

"Yes. Did you find out anything more?"

"We were at the Ruiz house most of the morning, then the lab. We had a short meeting with the DA, but after that we took some time to go to the hospital and check on Otero's condition."

The Ruiz family and the fingerprints on Manuel's birthday card took priority over the attack on Ramon Otero, Liz thought. Since detectives from the other precinct were investigating Ramon's case, Ike and Lou could step in on a limited basis only because Ramon's sister was Manuel's girlfriend.

"How's Ramon doing?" she asked.

"He's hanging on but still out of it."

"Sophie told me the department is on the alert for a big battle between the Serps and the Zumas if he doesn't make it."

"Right. The chief's trying to arrange a meeting of gang leaders to avert it. Well, I'll see you tonight. You want to go somewhere to eat?"

She didn't want to wait until after they came back from a restaurant dinner to start talking freely about Manuel's murder, Ramon's stabbing, and the threat of a major gang war.

"No, I'll get something at the grocery store on my way home," she replied.

"Hey, this is *good.*" Ike said at his first taste of the barbecued chicken Liz had whipped up. "Not that I'm surprised," he added—somewhat hastily, Liz thought. "You're getting to be a great cook."

He raised his wine goblet, saying, "Here's to your cooking prowess."

"Thanks," she replied, feeling pleased with herself and grateful to Gram, who'd told her about a certain brand of bottled barbecue sauce. It cost more than the others, but now she knew it was well worth it.

But, as happy as she was that the meal had made a hit with Ike, a discussion of her improved cooking skills was not on her agenda. Among the many questions she needed to ask were, had he and Lou Sanchez found Manuel's note in Grandmother Ruiz's knitting basket, and what else had kept them so busy all day?

Ike answered before she asked. "I'm surprised you haven't questioned me about the note in the knitting basket. We found it."

"I was just about to bring that up. How did the grandmother react?"

"She shed some tears, but we could tell she was a lot happier than she was before. The kids were all in school, and Gina and Carlos were at work when we got there. Yolanda was very pleased about the note too. We spent some time with her and the grandmother, hoping to get some more insight into the night of the murder. Then Carlos came home for lunch, and we talked with him for a while too."

"How did Carlos react when you told him Manuel had come back to the house to make peace with his grandmother?"

"He seemed genuinely surprised and pleased, and when we showed him the note, he got emotional." Ike paused, looking into her eyes. "Liz, I might as well tell you now, we're easing off the Ruiz family."

"You mean you've ruled them all out?"

He hesitated. "Well, not totally. There are still possible suspects within the family, but so far we've found nothing to connect them to Manuel's murder."

"What about those unclear fingerprints on the birthday card?"

Ike speared another piece of chicken from the serving dish, saying, "The technicians have gone as far as they can with those prints. They've tested what they have against all the prints we got at the Ruiz house."

Liz felt confused. Ike was being evasive, and it seemed obvious he wasn't going to tell her which members of the Ruiz family were still under suspicion. Maybe the long, drawn-out process at the lab had raised questions in his mind that he wasn't ready to share with her?

"When we went to the lab this afternoon, we found out that the technicians had lifted enough to determine that none of the prints on anything belong to *any* member of the Ruiz family," he continued. "An incomplete thumbprint from the birthday card showed a partial whorl in an unusual pattern not present in any of the prints taken from the Ruiz household. Although we're not ready to eliminate the entire Ruiz family, from now on we're concentrating on the possibility of a gang killing."

Liz thought of the Serp with the scarred chin. What if he had an unusual whorl on one of his thumbs?

"Wouldn't that partial thumbprint be enough for you to make an arrest?" she asked.

"No. There'd have to be a clear print of the entire thumb." He smiled. "Are you thinking the thumbprint might belong to that Serp you call Scarred Chin?"

She nodded. "Have you looked into his background?"

"Yeah. That's something else we did today. His name's Pepe Barboa. He has a record of two assaults with a deadly weapon—a stiletto. Got off one with a plea of self-defense.

Served some time for the second. He's only been out for a couple of months."

A stiletto! That seemed almost too obvious, Liz thought. "Does this make him a prime suspect in Manuel's murder—and maybe Ramon's stabbing too?" she asked.

"It definitely makes him a person of interest. His prints are on record, and they're being matched with the partials in the lab. We're holding off questioning him until Otero comes to and is able to talk."

"Did the doctors say there's a chance of that?"

"A good chance, they said. This wouldn't guarantee he's going to make it, but he might be able to identify his attacker."

"Did the detectives from the other squad mention fingerprints?"

"Yeah, they found Ramon's wallet and a switchblade in his pants pocket. If they'd been found in a trash bin like Manuel's wallet, at least there'd be a shot at picking up prints other than Ramon's. Evidently Otero never got a chance to use his switchblade before he was attacked. The wallet and knife are being held with his other personal effects in the other precinct."

"Ramon is rumored to be a drug dealer. Hasn't he ever been arrested?" Liz asked.

"According to narcotics, he's an extremely clever operator. They've been trying for some time to get the goods on him, but so far he has a clean record."

"Did the detectives on the other squad go through his wallet?"

"Yeah. Nothing incriminating, they said."

After they finished eating, Ike suggested they take their coffee to their new apartment. "I think we can get along without watching the news for a little while," he said. "If there's anything new, Lou will call me."

"Good idea," Liz replied. She put their coffee mugs onto a tray, and they headed for the door.

In the hallway outside their future home, she said, "We should spend as much time as possible here, so you can get used to it. You've been living in that bachelor pad for a long time. I don't want you to feel strange when we move in here."

He gave her a quick kiss. "Living with you, I know I'll have many feelings, but 'strange' isn't one of them."

Liz returned the kiss. Not all Ike's compliments were flowery, but they were always satisfying.

In the apartment, she glanced around with a pleased smile. Joe only had to install new window blinds, and he'd be finished working on it. All their new furniture had been delivered and set up. The tan leather sofa and matching chairs, the walnut tables, and the white pottery lamps all looked great with the freshly-painted, off-white walls. When Gram's colorful needlepoint pillows were placed on the sofa, the Oriental patterned rug on the hardwood floor, and the other, old, familiar pieces added, this place would look and feel like home.

While she and Ike were on their honeymoon, Joe was going to attend to the finishing touches and then move her old furnishings in. She'd already put some of her clothing and personal items into the bedroom closet and one of the chests and made up the king-size bed with beautiful, beige, silky-smooth sheets—a shower gift from Sophie's mother. With the handsome white spread, hand-crocheted by Gram, topping the bed, and walnut tables and matching lamps flanking it, the bedroom, like the living room, exuded an aura of comfort and understated elegance.

With a sigh of contentment, she put the tray onto the coffee table and settled herself on the sofa. "Everything looks wonderful. Makes me want to move in right away."

"Me too," Ike said. "I know that's out, but Joe's almost done, and there's no reason *you* shouldn't move in yourself. Why don't you?"

She looked at him, startled for a few moments, before deciding his question made sense. "That's a good idea," she replied. "I'll talk to Joe about it tomorrow."

The move wouldn't take Joe long, she thought. She could

help with small items. The more she thought about it, the better she liked it.

"In a few days I could be cooking dinner in our nice, big kitchen," she said.

"I know Joe's a man of action," he replied. "You could be using our new stove sooner than you expected. That delicious barbecued chicken might have been our last dinner in your old place."

She laughed. "You're right about Joe. He'll probably want to get on it immediately. But I want to help him, and I won't be able to do that tomorrow. I'm going to Staten Island in the morning, and I'll be with Gram until sometime in the afternoon."

"What are you and Gram up to tomorrow?"

"I'm having the final fitting on my wedding gown." She cast him a teasing smile. "Your bachelor days are numbered, Detective Eichle."

He raised his coffee mug, saying, "Here's to number zero."

Later, after they'd kissed good night and she was snuggled into her sofa bed, it struck her that while they were in their new apartment tonight, they hadn't discussed Manuel's murder as fully as they usually did. The prospect of her move had diverted both of them.

But now she was too sleepy to do any mental sleuthing. She'd get back to it again tomorrow.

Chapter Eighteen

With the final fitting of her wedding gown on her mind, as well as her decision to start living in the new apartment as soon as possible, Liz got up earlier than she generally did on Saturdays. Before she left for Staten Island, she wanted to consult with Joe and find out how soon he could move her out of the old place and into the new.

On her way out, she knocked on the Moscarettis' door. Joe answered it.

"I can do it anytime, Liz," he said, when she asked him about the move. "Today, if you want. It won't take long. The only big piece you have is your sofa bed."

The idea of moving in today delighted her. "Oh, I'd love to do it today, but I'm going to Gram's, and I'll be there most of the afternoon."

"You don't need to be here. Remember, I was going to do it while you were on your honeymoon, anyway. So, what do you say?"

Liz felt a rush of excitement. "I say yes! Moving in today is a wonderful idea!" she exclaimed.

Just then Rosa joined them at the door, saying. "Did I hear you say you're going to move into your new place, today, dearie?"

"Yes. The more I think about it, the more I like the idea. I'm really excited about it. I can't wait to start living there!"

''I like the idea too, Rosa replied. "Why wait?"

"So I'll move you in today, Liz," Joe said. "When you get back from Staten Island, you can walk right in and start living in your new place. You want the big rug to go in the living room in front of your new couch, and the old sofa bed goes in the little room where Ike's going to put his computer, right?"

"Right." Liz pictured herself coming back from Gram's and finding all her old, cherished possessions in place among the furnishings she and Ike had selected together. Her spirits soared to new heights—until she noticed a slight frown on Rosa's face.

"Joe, I just thought of something. I don't want you moving that big, heavy sofa bed all by yourself," Rosa said. "You're not a kid anymore. You want to end up with a bad back or, worse, a heart attack?"

Liz nodded. "Rosa's right, Joe. Could you get someone to help you with it?"

"Yes. Why don't you call that kid down the block who helped you move the old refrigerator into the basement?" Rosa suggested.

"Freddie?" Joe shook his head. "I was talking to his father a couple of days ago. He said the whole family's going away for the weekend."

"It's going to be hard to get anyone else on a weekend," Rosa said.

Joe cast Liz regretful look. "Sorry. But I'll get Freddie to come after school on Monday. Your place will be ready when you come home from work."

Rosa's eyes reflected Liz's disappointment. "I'm sorry too, dearie," she said, patting Liz's shoulder. "You had your heart set on moving today, didn't you?"

Coming down from her pink cloud, Liz tried to hide her feelings. "It's okay," she replied, managing a smile. "Today or Monday—what's the difference?"

The difference was, she had, indeed, set her heart on today. Feeling let down, she went on her way.

On the subway and ferry, the feeling lingered. *Snap out of it,* she told herself. *Stop being childish—like a kid denied a coveted treat.* She'd be living in her new apartment in another two days anyway.

By the time she started walking from the train station to Gram's house, much of her disappointment had ebbed away, and when she passed by Our Lady Queen of Peace church, a feeling of nostalgia took over. This old church had been and always would be an important part of her life.

As far back as she could remember, she'd gone here to Sunday Mass. Here she'd attended parochial school. Here, in first grade, she and Sophie Pulaski had found each other and formed the friendship they both knew would be everlasting. Here they'd made their first Communion together. Here as a bridesmaid, she'd stood near the altar, while Sophie and Ralph pledged themselves to each other. And here, two weeks from today, she and Ike would exchange their marriage vows.

Approaching Gram's house, she noticed a small truck parked in the driveway. If it was a repairman's truck, she hoped that whatever the problem was, it could be solved within a few days. With the wedding reception being held here in only two Saturdays, this was no time for something like a failed heating system or a leaking roof.

Gram must have been watching for her from the front window. Before Liz got halfway to the porch steps, the front door swung open, and Gram appeared, all smiles.

"After you try on the gown, we'll have lunch," she said, as they hugged. "How long can you stay?"

"I want to make the three o'clock ferry. Ike's picking me up."

"Good. We'll have time for a nice, long talk."

Stepping into the front hall, Liz saw a paint-spattered drop cloth on the floor along with buckets, brushes, and other implements of a housepainter's trade.

"Oh, I see there's some redecoration in progress," she said.

Gram nodded. "I'm having the downstairs done in a lovely light beige color like I saw on a TV home-decorating show."

"When I saw the truck outside, I was afraid you had a repair problem, like a flooded basement or something."

"Thank goodness nothing like that is likely to happen,"

Gram replied, leading the way up the stairs to the sewing room. "I just had the whole house inspected to make sure everything's in good shape, especially the plumbing. And the garage too. No use taking chances the garage roof might spring a leak. When Mr. Hagermeyer is done with the painting, he's going to move some of the living room furniture out there so there'll be more room in the house for the reception."

"All this for me," Liz said. "Thanks, Gram."

"I couldn't have my only granddaughter's wedding reception with dingy walls," Gram replied.

In the sewing room, the first thing that caught Liz's eye was the wedding gown, first worn by Sophie's mother, and then by Sophie, spread out on the daybed next to Gram's sewing machine, its ivory satin and lace as beautiful now as when Mrs. Pulaski was the bride. Seeing it made her feel happier than ever that she was going to wear it.

"The last time you were here, I noticed it needed to be taken in some more around the waist," Gram said, helping Liz into the gown. "I finished doing that. Now we'll see if it's ready to go."

Looking at her reflection in the full-length mirror, Liz felt a rush of emotion. Next time she put on the gown would be her wedding day.

"It's perfect," she said.

"And the veil was perfect when you tried it on last time you were here," Gram replied. "We're all set."

She assisted Liz out of the gown, saying, "The next two weeks are going to fly by. Do you think Ike will have the Ruiz murder solved before the wedding?"

"I don't know, Gram. He doesn't let me in on everything, but he did tell me he thinks there's a good chance it will be wrapped up before the big day."

"I know you'd enjoy your honeymoon even more with the case solved."

Liz nodded. "With Ike and Lou putting in extra time on it, I feel optimistic."

"I've thought, all along, it was a gangland killing," Gram

replied. "I saw a program on TV about how some gangs are getting very vicious—even murdering their own members for breaking gang rules. Maybe the senator's son broke one of their rules."

"Manuel Ruiz *did* break one of his gang's rules," Liz said.

She told Gram about her meeting with Dolores Otero and the forbidden romance. "But it's hard to believe he was murdered because he wouldn't break up with her," she said.

"After seeing that program on TV about gangs, it's not hard for *me* to believe it," Gram replied. She gave Liz an intuitive look. "Did anything else happen after the funeral?"

"I was getting to that. I have so much more to tell you, I hardly know where to begin."

Gram's eyes sparkled in anticipation. "Let's go down to the kitchen," she said. "You can tell me everything while we're having lunch."

Later, when Liz got off the boat at South Ferry, Ike was waiting for her in the Taurus.

"So, how's your Gram, and how did it go with the dress?" Ike asked, giving her a kiss.

"Gram's fine, and so's the wedding gown. What have *you* been doing all day? I know you're supposed to be off, but I suppose you've been putting in overtime on the case."

She saw the suggestion of a smile on his face as he turned the Taurus north onto Broadway. "Not today," he replied.

Easing up on the Ruiz family had taken some of the pressure off, she thought. Now he could concentrate, fully, on the gang angle. She was about to question him about Scarred Chin's fingerprints, when he asked her if she'd spoken to Joe about moving into their new apartment as soon as possible.

"Yes. He was going to do it today, but he decided to wait until he could get someone to help with the sofa bed."

Her reply seemed to amuse him. "Good thing he did. That monster's too much for him to handle alone," he said with a laugh.

"I know, but I'd gotten all revved up about coming home

from Gram's today and finding everything settled in our new place. I was really disappointed. I know it's silly, but I still feel a bit down."

"I'll try to fix that," he said with a broad smile.

When Ike parked the Taurus near the Moscarettis' brownstone, Liz found herself wishing, again, that they could bypass the door to her present apartment and go into the one where they'd soon be living together. In her mind's eye, she could plainly see the living room, all cozied up with the colorful, Persian style rug and needlepoint pillows Gram had given her, and the familiar old accessories Mom had donated when she and Pop moved to Florida. She knew Ike would have been as pleased as she.

They went up the stairway. Key in hand, Liz headed for her apartment. But Ike took her arm and guided her past it, saying, "Wrong door."

Even when he opened the door to the other apartment, she still didn't get it. It wasn't until she saw Gram's needlepoint pillows on the sofa, the Persian style rug under the coffee table, and Rosa and Joe coming out of the kitchen, that she understood. For a moment all she could do was look at the three of them, one after the other, speechless with surprise.

"Now you know what I did today," Ike said with a big smile.

"Everything's in, right down to your toothbrush," Rosa said. "And I brought up a box of pasta and made clam sauce for your dinner. The sauce is in your new fridge, ready to be heated up in your new microwave."

"And Ike and I got your TV hooked up to the cable," Joe added.

Liz had barely recovered from her surprise long enough to thank them all, when Joe turned toward the door, saying, "Come on, Rosa, let's leave these two lovebirds to enjoy their future home."

When the door closed behind them, Ike took Liz into his arms. "Are you happy?" he asked.

"Ecstatic!" She followed up with a kiss and then a question. "Did Joe call you and ask you to help him? Did he tell you I was acting like a big baby because I couldn't move in today?"

"No. *I* called *him* and told him I was available. Last night, after I left here, I got to thinking about it. I knew you wanted to move in ASAP, and I thought it was a great idea." He glanced around the room. "Everything looks okay, doesn't it?"

"Yes." She snuggled closer to him. "Thank you for being so thoughtful. You and Joe did a great job. Everything's perfect."

He shook his head. "Not quite," he said.

She looked at him in puzzlement. "Why?"

He faked a look of chagrin. "This move didn't include *me*. I'm feeling a bit down about it."

"To quote someone I love dearly, 'I'll try to fix that,' " she said.

From that moment on, all thoughts of murder and stabbings and fingerprints and gangs were temporarily forgotten.

Chapter Nineteen

When Liz woke up the next morning, it took her a few minutes to realize she was in the new apartment. That was partly because she'd spent the night in her old sofa bed, in the little room off the kitchen. She wanted to wait until she and Ike came home from their honeymoon before she slept in the king-size bed they'd picked out together.

The apartment looked even better in the morning than it had last night, she thought while brewing her morning coffee. She reveled in its ample space—the large bathroom and kitchen with plenty of storage, and the big clothes closets. And that extra room off the kitchen added to the livability. She pictured Ike's computer in there instead of set up in a corner of the bedroom or living room. And with her old sofa bed in there, it could double as guest quarters. At that moment she felt as if she'd moved into a mansion.

Gram had been right when she said the next two weeks would fly by. So many things to attend to within so short a time.

One evening that week, while Sophie's husband, Ralph, was working, she and Sophie were going to hit the resort-wear departments of a few stores. She needed shorts and tees for the Bahamas.

"And you gotta get a really knockout bikini," Sophie had said.

Also, she needed to set aside time to shop for her wedding gift to Ike. She wanted the gift to be something special. It might take some prolonged searching to find it.

Friday evening, she and Ike had a meeting scheduled with Father Flynn and Pastor Drucker, the two clergymen who were going to perform their ecumenical marriage service. And Saturday night, members of Ike's squad were throwing him a bachelor party at a favorite NYPD gathering place, while she and her female friends partied at a Rockefeller Center restaurant.

She was taking most of the following week off from work to attend to a flurry of last-minute details, including checking with the florist, helping Gram get her house into order, plus other preparations for the reception, standing by for the arrival of Ike's parents, Aunt Hilda, and Pop and Mom, and going for a special hairdo at Nick's Crowning Glory.

Suddenly it struck her that the distraction of wedding details and plans for moving had taken over her mind. She hadn't thought much about Pepe Barboa or Ramon Otero since yesterday. Barboa's fingerprints were on record. Had they been tested against the prints on Manuel Ruiz's birthday card? Had Ramon regained consciousness? She'd get answers when Ike came over that afternoon. They were going for another walk in Central Park.

"This time just for the pleasure of being together in Manhattan's great outdoors," Ike had said.

Remembering their last walk in the park and how Uncle Carlos had dealt with the paparazzi, she knew it would take her a while to get used to easing off the Ruiz family members as suspects in Manuel's murder. But switching from them to a possible gang murder wouldn't be too difficult. She'd already given it some thought. If Pepe Barboa wasn't the actual killer, he was probably the ringleader.

She and Rosa went to nine o'clock Mass. Afterward they both noticed that the weather had turned cold and blustery—not ideal for a walk in the park.

She phoned Gram, Mom and Pop, and then Sophie, to tell them about her move. Later Ike called, asking how she liked being in the new place.

"It's wonderful," she replied. "And I loved having breakfast in our big kitchen this morning. I wish you could have been here with me."

"Me too." He paused. "Liz, I'm sorry, but our walk in the park this afternoon is out. I'll be over this evening, though."

She quelled her curiosity. He'd tell her tonight what had come up. "Coming back from Mass, I noticed it was getting cold and windy. It probably wouldn't have been a good day for our walk, anyway," she said.

"Yeah, I caught a weather report on the car radio. It mentioned we might get the fringes of a snowstorm from the New England area later on," Pausing, he added, "I'll bring takeout for dinner tonight, okay?"

"Wouldn't you like a home-cooked meal?"

"Sure, I would."

"Okay, then. I'm going to the market as soon as we hang up and get the fixings for beef stew."

She'd been trying to improve .her cooking skills, and Gram's recipe for Irish stew was one of the meals she knew she was good at.

"Gram's Irish stew? Great. I'll see you around six."

"You're not getting any Irish stew till you tell me why you had to cancel our walk in the park," Liz said the instant Ike stepped into the apartment.

"You drive a hard bargain," he replied, giving her a hug and a kiss. "I didn't want to take Lou away from his family on a Sunday, so I went, by myself, to Dolores Otero's home to interview her and her mother."

That hadn't been included in Liz's speculations. She looked at him in surprise. "Didn't detectives from the other squad already interview them?"

He nodded. "Let's get started on dinner, and I'll tell you all about it."

In the kitchen, while he poured their wine and she gave the stew a final stir, he filled her in on the interview.

"The attack on Ramon took place in another precinct, and the detectives on that squad interviewed Mrs. Otero and Dolores, hoping to get information that might help in identifying the assailant. But with the relationship between Ramon's sister and a man murdered in my precinct, I have a different slant on it."

Of course, Liz thought. He wanted to question Dolores and perhaps pick up something that might incriminate another Serp member in Manuel's murder. Dolores might have remembered something Manuel had said about one of them. While she filled their bowls with stew, an image of Pepe Barboa's mean eyes and scarred chin flashed into her mind.

When they sat down at the table in the kitchen alcove, she waited expectantly for Ike to give her the full details of the interview.

"Dolores couldn't have been more cooperative," he began.

"Wasn't her mother cooperative?" Liz asked.

"Mrs. Otero didn't say much, but I think that was because most of my questions were directed to Dolores. Unfortunately, I didn't pick up anything new in that area. If Manuel had any fears about one of his gang members, he didn't confide them to her."

Liz felt a pang of disappointment. It sounded as if the interview hadn't accomplished anything.

"I'm sorry it didn't work out," she said.

"It wasn't a total waste of time," he replied. "The little Mrs. Otero had to say got me thinking and raised some questions. She said she and her husband came here from Mexico when their children were very young. I want to interview her again and get more details."

Liz looked at him, somewhat puzzled. "Dolores told me she and Ramon weren't even in school yet when they came here. But why should that raise questions?"

"Judging from the approximate present ages of Dolores and Ramon, the family came from Mexico about twelve years ago," Ike continued. "And yet their mother speaks fluent English with no trace of an accent. Lou and I have encountered many Mexican immigrants who've been here far longer and don't speak English half as well, if they speak it at all."

Liz nodded. "Dolores told me their mother spoke fluent English, but her father spoke only Spanish. After her father died, her mother went to night school and took business courses so she could get a better job."

"She must have been speaking English like an American when she took those business courses. Makes me wonder what sort of school she went to in Mexico."

Liz looked at him in puzzlement. "Am I missing something here? What does Mrs. Otero's fluency in English have to do with Manuel Ruiz's murder?"

"Could be nothing," he replied. "It just struck me as something I should look into."

When Ike was struck with a hunch, it generally led to something, Liz thought. But even her wildfire imagination couldn't make anything out of this one.

He took his first taste of the stew and followed up with a smile. "This is even better than the last time you made it."

"Thanks. Must be the new stove."

He didn't seem to be in any hurry to fill her in on the latest lab results or Ramon Otero's condition. She waited until he'd taken a few more mouthfuls before broaching the subjects.

"Anything new on the birthday card fingerprints?"

"Nope, still no match."

There'd be no mistaking that unusual whorl he'd mentioned, she thought. Again, Pepe Barboa came to mind. His fingerprints were on record. Had they been matched against the partial prints on the birthday card?

When she asked him, Ike nodded. "Yeah. They came up zilch."

That seemed to indicate that the scarred-chinned Serp wasn't Manuel's killer. Liz quelled her disappointment.

"How about Ramon's condition?" she asked. "Did Dolores and her mother seem optimistic?"

"Yeah. He's still unconscious, but today the doctor told them it looks like he's going to make it."

Good, Liz thought, and not only for the sake of Dolores and her mother. She hadn't forgotten what both Sophie and Ike had told her. If Ramon died, the Zumas would blame the

Serps and want revenge. Other gangs might take sides. Manhattan could be plunged into a gang war.

They finished eating and took their coffee into the living room—their usual routine, only in a brand-new setting.

"This really feels like home," Ike said, settling onto their new couch and looking around at all the familiar things from Liz's old place, combined with the new furnishings they'd picked out together.

He glanced at her small TV on a nearby table, adding, "All we need is one of those oversized screens we've been talking about."

He was the one who'd been talking about a huge-screen TV, Liz thought. She knew he really wanted to watch sports and his favorite World War II movies on it.

"Soon as we get back from our honeymoon, we'll look for one," she said.

At that moment, Ike's phone sounded. "It's Lou," he said, checking the caller ID.

She thought something had developed regarding the Ruiz case, and he'd have to leave, until she heard him say, "No, I haven't heard about it. We haven't been watching TV."

As Liz sprang to turn on a news channel, Ike clicked off the phone, saying, "A rumor's going around on the streets that Ramon Otero died this afternoon. According to the hospital, it's not true, but the Zumas and some other Mexican gangs are already out, massing for a conflict. Looks like we're in for a violent night."

Chapter Twenty

Liz's first thoughts were of Dolores and her mother. Had they heard the rumor? Was Dolores in danger?

"Do you think the Serps will go after Dolores, as part of their battle against the Zumas?" she asked.

Ike shook his head. "To do that, they'd have to invade Zuma territory. With the Zumas out in full force, I believe Dolores and her mother will be okay."

"Oh, good. But I hope they didn't hear the rumor."

"I think the hospital would have assured them that Ramon's still alive. But getting the word out to the gangs isn't going to be that easy."

How could the hospital let the gangs know the truth before the knifing and shooting started? Liz wondered. Even repeated news bulletins wouldn't do it. Zumas, Serps, and their respective allies weren't home watching TV. They were already out on the streets, angry, armed to the teeth, and itching for a fight. She pictured NYPD vehicles cruising with loudspeakers blaring: *Attention! We have an announcement from hospital officials. Ramon Otero did not die. Repeat. Ramon Otero is alive. . . .*

Ike had tuned in the news. Would he take a quick look at it and then tell her he had to cut their evening short?

Just then, a bulletin came on, announcing that Ramon Otero had not died, followed by a statement from the police commissioner, who described the situation as dangerous. Even though gang activity was presently confined to Manhattan, in an area west of Central Park, he warned residents of all sections of the city to keep off the streets.

That sounded serious, Liz thought. Any minute now, Ike might tell her he had to leave.

"I feel like a World War Two woman, about to send my man off to battle," she said." Do you have to go to the station house?"

He smiled and gave her a hug. "As in, 'All personnel report to their units'? No. Riot Control and mobilized officers will handle it."

His smile faded. "Let's hope the word gets out onto the streets that Ramon is alive, or, if it doesn't, let's pray that this can be put down without casualties."

Liz's house phone rang. "I'll bet that's Pop and Mom," she said. "The news must be on Florida TV too."

Caller ID confirmed her suspicion. Just as she picked up, Ike's cell phone sounded. "And *my* folks heard it too," he said.

By the time they'd finished talking with their respective parents, live coverage was on TV. Liz watched hordes of angry, shouting young men surging through dark streets. She recognized the purple and yellow beads of the Zumas predominating among the varied regalia of allied gangs. As yet she saw no sign of the Serps' orange and green bandanas. Instead of penetrating Zuma territory, were they lying in wait somewhere within their own turf, ready to confront any invaders?

"This is scary," she said with a shudder.

Ike nodded, frowning. "Looks to me like this is bigger than expected."

Above the loud shouts, they heard the voice of a TV photojournalist on the scene, practically repeating what Ike had just said. Moments later a bulletin came on with another statement from the police commissioner. More officers had been mobilized to control the huge numbers of gang members now on the march, and, just as Liz had imagined, police vehicles had been assigned to the streets, loudspeakers blaring that Ramon Otero was alive.

"I doubt if those loudspeakers will have much effect," Ike said. "They'll think it's just a police trick to get them off the streets."

Liz took their coffee mugs into the kitchen for refills. While there, she found herself imagining the police unable to prevent a large-scale riot.

"Do you think the cops can control this?" she asked, coming back.

A grim look crossed his face. "I honestly don't know. Nothing like this has ever happened in New York since I've been on the force."

And she'd never heard Pop talk about anything like this here, either.

"I didn't know there were quite so many gangs in the city," she said. "What if the cops are outnumbered and unable to control them?"

"The National Guard might have to be called in," he replied.

At that moment the photojournalist's voice took on an excited tone. "Here come the cops!"

Liz's heart bounded when she saw a line of NYPD officers in riot gear approaching, only to plummet when she noticed how few there were, compared to the number of Zumas and their allies. And when the Serps and their cohort gangs got into it, the situation would become even worse. Although she felt stirrings of uneasiness, she believed the well-trained officers of the NYPD could handle this disorganized mob.

Ike got to his feet and walked to the window. "So far this has been confined to an area on the Upper West Side," he said. "Let's hope it stays that way."

Liz joined him at the window. Below, everything looked normal. Traffic flowed as usual. Vehicle lights blended with the glow from surrounding buildings, and, despite the police commissioner's warning, pedestrians strolled the sidewalks.

That was understandable, she thought. Even her lively imagination couldn't picture a bloody gang battle spilling over into this part of the city.

"People aren't taking this seriously," she said. *Myself included,* she had to admit.

Just as she spoke, the TV reporter's voice crackled in her ears, sounding as sharp as the development he was reporting.

Las Serpientes had appeared on the scene, and the first shot had been fired!

She heard the reporter's voice, shrill and shaken. "The area is being evacuated, so—" When she turned to look at the screen, it had gone blank.

She stared at it. Suddenly her imagination went into action. The nebulous danger now loomed large and real. A chilling thought gripped her. Sophie's husband, Ralph Perillo, might be among the mobilized cops. She felt herself trembling.

Ike's arms closed around her. "It'll be okay, Liz," he said, his voice calm and steady.

How could he say that with such assurance? It was unnerving enough to know that the first shot had been fired in this senseless riot, but suppose that bullet had found its way into the heart of a cop?

Gently Ike turned her around to face the window. "Look," he said, "it's starting to rain."

Seeing raindrops pelting the glass, she shifted her gaze down onto the glistening street. She shook her head. Pedestrians were ducking for shelter, but it would take more than a little rain to douse the flaring tempers of the warring gangs.

"Rain can be tricky at this time of year," Ike said. "The temperature has dropped considerably since this afternoon. With a little luck, we could get sleet and ice. That might help cool down some of those hotheads."

He glanced toward the TV. Following his glance, Liz saw that the news channel had switched from live coverage to the studio, where commentators were discussing the escalation of hostilities. Apparently they were awaiting word from the reporter who'd so suddenly cut off coverage.

"Nothing new here," he said. "Let's try the other channels."

Changing channels provided only the same kind of studio reporting. Evidently live coverage at the scene had been suspended after the shooting started, Liz decided. Too dangerous for reporters and camerapeople.

Ike looked out the window again. "Looks like the rain's

not letting up," he said. "If it's as cold now as it was when I got here, it's gotta be miserable out there."

Liz knew he was trying to reassure her, trying to make her think the gangs would call off hostilities. Although she couldn't believe cold rain would possibly deter the angry ranks she'd seen on TV, she wished it would. If they postponed their battle until the weather broke, by that time the gangs might believe the reports that Dolores' brother hadn't died, and this frightening situation would end.

Again the thought plagued her that Ralph Perillo might have been mobilized. Although he was in detective training, maybe that wouldn't exempt him from such duty.

"Do you think Ralph could have been assigned to this?" she asked.

Her heart sank when Ike didn't answer immediately. When he did, his response seemed carefully composed. "I guess it depends on how many men are needed."

"I have to call Sophie," she said, picking up the phone.

Sophie answered after the first ring. Her voice sounded strained. "Oh, Liz, I know you're calling about Ralph. . . ."

"Is he out there, Sophie?"

"Not yet. He was put on the backup list. He left for the station house a few minutes ago."

"Oh, Sophie. I hope and pray it's over before he has to get into it. Ike says the bitter cold and rain might break it up."

"I wish I could believe that cold, rainy weather would drive those gangs off the streets, but after seeing them on TV . . ." Sophie's voice faltered. "They all looked so vicious, like they're out for blood. I know a cop's wife is expected to take these things in stride, but I'm scared, Liz."

Liz brushed at her eyes. She was scared too, but letting Sophie know that would only add to her worry about Ralph. They talked for a few minutes, with Liz doing her best to reassure Sophie.

After they said good-bye, Ike was still at the window. She reported what Sophie had told her about Ralph being put on reserve.

"That's good," Ike said. "Chances are, this weather is going to dampen the gangs' enthusiasm for battle, and the backups won't be sent in."

"Sophie doesn't think cold rain will keep the gangs from going at each other," Liz said. She tried not to blurt her next thought, but it came out anyway. "And neither do I."

He slid an arm around her and pointed out the window, saying, "How about snow?"

Looking out, she was surprised to see that the rain had turned into swirling white flakes. But would it come down heavily enough to make the gangs call it quits?

Ike must have noticed the dubious look on her face. "You can forget about saying a little flurry isn't going to bother the gangs," he said. "While you were talking to Sophie, I phoned the weather bureau for a local report. This is no flurry. The big snowstorm they thought would only graze the city is moving in."

Liz glanced out the window again. Sure, the snow was coming down thick and fast, but she'd seen many snowstorms where kids of all ages couldn't wait to start dragging their sleds outdoors. Why would this one drive hardened gang members indoors and put their intended warfare on hold?

"I can see you're not convinced," Ike said. "Well, maybe this will change your mind. After I got the report from the weather bureau, I checked it out on TV. Take a look."

She turned around. Onscreen a meteorologist was standing in front of a huge map of the United States, showing the east coast, from Maine to New Jersey, covered with white icons.

She listened to him describe the incorrectly predicted storm as a nor'easter, using words such as *massive, dangerous, monster, gale-force winds, severe impact,* and *blizzard conditions.*

"The fast-moving storm, which slammed into the New York City area a few minutes ago, is expected to last through the night and well into tomorrow," the meteorologist stated. He went on to forecast a record snowfall, along with bitter cold and high winds.

"I should call Gram and make sure she's okay," Liz said. "This snow started so suddenly. . . ." She pictured Gram, out somewhere, trying to make her way home through the storm.

To her great relief, Gram answered the phone. "I was out grocery shopping and got home just as it began to snow," she said. "It sounds like it's going to be as bad as the famous blizzard of 1888. I hope it is. A storm like that would take care of those street hoodlums. I hope it freezes their butts off."

After they said good-bye, Liz reported to Ike. "Gram hopes we're in for another blizzard of 1888." She repeated Gram's further comments.

Ike laughed. "Shall we check the news and find out if her hopes are materializing?" he asked.

On TV, all channels were reporting that the dreaded gang war had, indeed, succumbed to likely the worst snowstorm to hit New York in more than a hundred years. Commentators were telling viewers that moments after the first gunshot, a cold rain had begun to fall, quickly changing into heavy snow driven by a biting wind. Visibility on the streets soon became close to zero. Unable to see through the thick, swirling flakes and numbed by the bone-chilling cold, the combatants had gotten off the streets.

Viewers were also told that police on the scene reported no casualties during the brief conflict. Intermittent announcements were made that rumors of Ramon Otero's death were false.

"Evidently the lone shot missed its mark," Ike said.

Liz nodded. "And now that the gangs are off the streets, maybe they'll find out on TV that Ramon is alive."

They watched live coverage of rapidly accumulating snow on streets and sidewalks. Although cameras showed various locations around the city, there were few shots of any snow-removal equipment at work.

"How come there aren't more plows out?" Liz asked. Another glance at the TV screen answered her question. The storm had hit so suddenly and with such ferocity that by the time the snow-removal equipment was readied, the overwhelming accumulation had rendered much of it ineffectual.

"Imagine how this will be in the morning," she said.

"Yeah," Ike replied. "Everything at a standstill. Schools and businesses closed. Streets blocked . . ." He stepped to the window and looked out. "Guess I'd better head for home while the roads are still passable."

Just as he spoke, a spokesman for the mayor came on TV with an emergency announcement, an official order banning all private cars from city streets, effective immediately until further notice. Violators would be subject to arrest and steep fines. Only emergency vehicles would be allowed on the streets. No exceptions.

Liz looked at Ike, expecting him to say that the Taurus was an unmarked police car, and even though it didn't qualify as an emergency vehicle, he'd take a chance on getting away with it. Instead, he returned her look with a grin.

"Sounds like I'll have to spend the night here."

She barely had time to express her wholehearted approval, when her phone rang.

"Dearie," Rosa said, "we just heard the mayor's announcement. I'm getting our spare bedroom and bathroom ready for Ike."

Chapter Twenty-one

When Liz awakened in the morning and tried to turn on her bedside lamp, it didn't work. *The bulb's burned out,* she thought, but a moment later she remembered the storm and wondered if it had caused a power outage. Throwing on her robe, she made her way to the window and looked out.

Not a glimmer of light shone in the dark, silent desert of white. Wind-driven snow was still falling, drifting, piling up on the abandoned street and sidewalks. She gazed at it, almost in awe. Ike was right when he said the city would come to a standstill overnight.

Her cell phone sounded. Probably Ike, still sacked out in Rosa and Joe's spare room. She dug the phone out of her purse and answered.

"Good morning, Detective."

"Good morning, Redlocks. I took a chance you'd be awake. Have you checked the weather yet?"

"Yes. Looks like it's not letting up. And I think the power's gone off."

"Yeah, it has, and most telephone service too. Lou woke me with his mobile a few minutes ago. He was up very early, and when he discovered that his apartment had no juice, he suspected there'd been a power failure. He called the station house and was told there's an outage affecting most of the city. It must have happened fairly recently. My room's still pretty warm. How's the apartment?"

"It feels comfortable. Are Rosa and Joe up yet?"

"Yeah, I hear them. They probably think I'm still asleep. I'll let them know I'm awake and get back to you."

He called again a few minutes later. "Rosa says to come on down. Breakfast will be ready in about twenty minutes."

Enough time for a shower while the water's still hot and the apartment's still warm, Liz thought. Grabbing her flashlight, she smiled at the prospect of a typical Rosa breakfast. Lucky the Moscarettis had a gas stove. Although it was still dark, she knew how resourceful Joe was. He'd have battery lanterns rigged up all over the house.

After she showered, she noticed that the apartment was getting chilly. She put on her warmest clothes—old brown woolen pants and flannel shirt from her college days, tan cardigan sweater, and heavy socks and loafers. And she remembered to tuck her cell phone into the pocket of her cardigan.

On her way to the door she thought of taking an extra sweater with her, until she remembered that the Moscarettis had two wood-burning fireplaces, one in their bedroom and the other in what they called their front room. *Thank heaven for the amenities in Manhattan's old brownstones!* Rosa and Joe used the fireplace in the front room often. She had no doubt that Joe had them both going this morning.

Ike greeted her at the Moscarettis' door with a kiss and a mug of steaming coffee. Instead of his usual coat and tie, he had on a heavy woolen sweater. Liz guessed it was one of Joe's.

"Looks like we're both dressed for the occasion," she said.

"Yeah. This sweater's part of Joe's emergency equipment, along with his battery-powered lanterns," Ike replied.

Rosa's voice sounded from the kitchen. "Go into the front room, dearie. Breakfast's ready. We'll eat in there by the fire instead of the dining room."

Liz glanced into the kitchen, where Rosa and Joe, both layered in sweaters, were dishing up scrambled eggs, bacon, hash brown potatoes, and biscuits.

"What can I do to help, Rosa?"

"Not a thing. Joe and I will bring the food in on trays."

Moments later they were all gathered around a blazing log fire.

Cuddled next to Ike on the sofa, Liz warmed her hands on the coffee mug, enjoying every comforting sip. Breakfast had never tasted so good. How lucky they were to be snug and warm and well fed.

She thought of all the people who weren't so lucky—the homeless, or those trapped in apartments with no heat, and those who hadn't made it to the grocery store before the storm started. There must be thousands of cold, hungry New Yorkers this morning.

"How are families with babies going to get through this?" she asked. "And elderly people and sick people, and the homeless?"

"If the power isn't restored pretty soon, there'll be a gigantic problem," Ike replied. "Eventually, if necessary, the police and firefighters will evacuate infants and the elderly and other vulnerable people in frigid apartments or on the street and get them into buildings with emergency generators—like hospitals, government buildings, and the armories." He shook his head. "The city has a fleet of all-terrain vehicles, including snowmobiles, but many of the cops and firefighters needed to operate them are snowed in at home and not yet able to report for duty. We weren't prepared for a storm of this magnitude. All we can do is hope it blows over soon and the plows can make some headway."

Joe went to the window and opened the blinds. In the gray daylight, snow still lashed the pane. "Looks like it's not going to stop anytime soon," he said.

Liz thought of Gram. She always kept plenty of food on hand, and there was a fireplace in her living room, but did she have enough firewood, and was her phone working?

When she called on her cell, she was relieved when Gram answered. Her phone was working, at least for now, and she sounded unworried.

"What a blizzard! I'm feeding breakfast to some neighbors and their kids. They were low on food yesterday and couldn't get out to the grocery. I'm sure *you're* not going hungry—not with the Moscarettis right downstairs."

"That's where I am now, toasting my toes at their fireplace and enjoying a super breakfast," Liz replied. "I knew you'd have plenty of food in the house, and now I know your phone's okay, but there's no telling how long the power outage will last. Do you have enough logs to keep your fireplace going through this?"

"Power outage?" Gram sounded surprised.

"You mean your electricity didn't go off?"

"Not that I noticed. The house is warm, and the lights are on, and I used my electric coffeemaker."

Liz laughed. "I guess it's safe to assume the outage didn't affect Staten Island."

"So far, so good," Gram said. "I hope it doesn't hit us over here. I'm too old to chop wood in a blizzard."

"I'm thankful you're okay, Gram, and everything's working."

"Everything but the TV. I guess the storm knocked out the cable. I'll miss my soap operas today."

"Let's hope it comes back before you miss too many episodes," Liz said. *And that Manhattan's power comes back before* I *miss too many news broadcasts,* she thought. But even if power was restored soon, how could television programming be resumed, with most newscasters and commentators snowbound in their homes? Even if a few of them made it to their studios, with communications at a standstill, how would they get any news to report?

Already she missed news coverage of Manuel Ruiz's murder. And she missed hearing Ike describe his ideas and his progress on the case. With the city tied up by the blizzard, his investigation had come to a halt.

Ike's voice penetrated her thoughts. "You're very quiet all of a sudden."

"I was thinking about the Ruiz case and wondering when you'll be able to resume your investigation."

"Lou and I aren't waiting for the storm to stop," he replied.

While she looked at him in surprise, he continued. "I've

been doing a lot of thinking about Mrs. Otero. I want to interview her again as soon as possible. When Lou called earlier, I discussed this with him, and we decided to do it this morning. She won't be at work, and there'll be no chance of interruptions."

Questions crowded Liz's mind. Why was another interview with Mrs. Otero so urgent? Why couldn't they wait until the weather cleared, instead of rushing to the Otero apartment in the midst of the worst blizzard in more than a century?

Before she could express her feelings, Rosa glanced out the window at the unabated snow and spoke up.

"Excuse me, Ike, but that sounds crazy. How would you get there?"

Joe nodded and chimed in. "Even if you could manage to drive there in this mess, your car's buried under six feet of snow." He laughed. "What you need is a snowmobile."

"That's exactly what we're going to use," Ike said. "I'm expecting another call from Lou. He lives only a few blocks from the precinct garage. He's done a lot of cross-country skiing, and he still has his equipment. As soon as he can get over there and get hold of one of the department's big, two-man snowmobiles, he's coming for me."

He looked at Joe with a grin. "Can you fix me up with some arctic gear?"

"Sure," Joe replied. "Come down to the basement with me, and we'll see what we can find."

Watching them leave the room, Liz had a skeptical moment. Riding across town through a blizzard on a snowmobile called for more than a wool cap and a couple of sweaters. Shaking her head, she looked at Rosa.

"Don't worry, dearie," Rosa said. "Joe never throws anything out. Besides his Marine things from Vietnam, he still has his father's World War Two army stuff in the basement. I got tired of keeping at him to get rid of it."

She poured more coffee into Liz's mug, adding, "Joe's father served in Europe. He was in the Battle of the Bulge."

The Battle of the Bulge. Besides old movies, Liz had seen many World War II documentaries on TV. Ike would be outfitted from head to toe with whatever it had taken to keep American troops warm during those fearful, brutally cold weeks of December 1944 and January 1945.

When Ike appeared a little while later, she appraised him with a smile. "You look as if you just stepped out of an old World War Two movie," she told him. "I think Spencer Tracy wore a cap like that in one of his films—earmuffs and all."

"And get the boots," Ike replied. "They were a little too big, so I put on two layers of woolen socks. No chance of frostbitten toes."

"Everything else fits pretty good too," Joe said with a broad smile. Liz knew he was pleased to have his sentimental treasures put to use.

At that moment, Ike's phone sounded. He brought it out of the pocket of his GI jacket. "That'll be Lou, saying he's on his way."

After a brief exchange, he clicked off, reporting the latest conditions.

The city sounded like photos Liz had seen on the weather channel of that legendary blizzard of 1888. All the modern miracles, all the wonderful technological progress made since then were still nearly powerless against the forces of nature.

Lou Sanchez arrived, his stocky frame, dressed in skiwear, looking far more up-to-date than Ike. But he admitted that his trip across town hadn't been much fun.

"But getting over to the west side again won't be quite as bad," he said. "We'll have the wind at our backs."

After he warmed himself at the hearth for a few minutes and drank some coffee, he looked at Ike with a grin. "Ready to go, soldier?"

"All set," Ike replied, putting on his GI cap and gloves.

He gave Liz a hug and a kiss and told her he'd phone her

after the interview was over. Rosa handed him a Thermos of coffee, Joe wished them luck, and they were off.

From the window, Liz watched them disappear beyond a thick curtain of blowing snow. Again she asked herself why Ike considered another interview with Mrs. Otero so urgent.

Chapter Twenty-two

Joe joined Liz at the window, saying, "Looks like Ike and Lou have a hot clue in the Ruiz murder. They wouldn't be out in this storm for nothing."

"I heard Ike say they wanted to interview somebody for a second time," Rosa said. "A Mrs. Otero, wasn't it, dearie?"

"Right," Liz replied.

"Otero. Isn't that the name of the gang member I heard about on TV who was stabbed the other night?" Joe asked.

The Moscarettis didn't know how involved she was in Ike's cases. But, since Ike had made no secret of where he and Lou were going and why, Liz saw no reason to be evasive.

"Yes, Mrs. Otero is the second stabbing victim's mother," she replied.

"His mother!" Rosa exclaimed. "What's she got to do with Manuel Ruiz's murder?"

"Maybe Ike thinks Manuel's killer might be the same guy who stabbed Otero, and he believes the mother might know more about the stabbing than she told him the first time," Joe replied. "Maybe she was afraid to talk, and Ike thinks he can change her mind."

Liz nodded. Joe had arrived at much the same conclusion as she.

"But why did they have to rush over there in a blizzard?" Rosa asked. "Why couldn't they have waited till the weather cleared?"

Rosa's question was the same as the one Liz had been

asking herself, from the moment Ike announced what he and Lou were going to do.

Again, Joe provided an answer. "If they waited till the weather cleared, Mrs. Otero might be at her job, and maybe they want to interview her in the privacy of her home instead of at work," he said.

That made as much sense as anything Liz could think of, but it still didn't fully explain the urgency.

Rosa headed for the kitchen, saying she was going to start making minestrone for lunch. Joe brought in more logs from the back stoop and busied himself at the fireplace.

Watching the snowflakes brush against the windowpane, Liz thought of Mom and Pop. If news of the storm and the gang violence had reached Florida, they must be worried. They'd have trouble reaching her by phone. Even cell service might be jammed by other anxious callers.

She tried to reach them via her cell but without success. She was right—all the circuits were busy. She'd try again later. Then she called Gram to reassure her, in case she'd heard about the gang violence and was worried.

A few minutes later Sophie phoned, sounding upbeat. "Hi, Liz."

"I guess that cheery voice means Ralph's with you," Liz replied.

"Yeah. Thank goodness he made it back here last night. Once the snow closed in and the gangs gave up, the backups weren't needed. Are you all right?"

"Yes, except I have no heat in my apartment. I guess you're in the same predicament."

"Right. Lucky we have a gas stove. We were able to make breakfast this morning. We're huddled in the kitchen, drinking hot coffee. How about you?"

"I'm cozy and warm by Rosa and Joe's fireplace."

"Good. Have you heard from Ike this morning? Did he have any trouble getting back to his apartment last night?"

Liz could not resist teasing her. "Last night we heard the

mayor's announcement banning all driving except emergency vehicles, so he couldn't leave."

"Oh?" Sophie's voice was a blend of speculation and excitement. "Are you saying he had to spend the night?"

"Yes—in the Moscarettis' spare room."

Sophie gave a hearty laugh. "I should have known! But at least the two of you are keeping warm by Rosa and Joe's fireplace."

"Not exactly. Ike's off to do a second interview with Ramon Otero's mother."

"What! In this storm? How . . . ?"

Liz described the snowmobile foray. "I think Ike believes that whoever attacked Ramon might be Manuel's killer. And I think he suspects that Mrs. Otero or Dolores might know more than they told him the first time around."

Sophie's reaction was predictable. "But what's so urgent about that? Couldn't the interview have waited? Why did they have to rush over there in a blizzard, on a snowmobile?"

"He must expect to pick up something important," Liz replied. "But I can't imagine what it could be."

"When *your* imagination can't come up with anything, it must be something far out," Sophie said. "Well, I gotta go. Ralph's getting ready to check the other apartments and see if they need anything. We did a a lot of grocery shopping on Saturday, so we have extras of everything, and the fridge hasn't been off long enough for anything to spoil. There's a baby across the hall who might need milk. Before Ralph leaves, I want to tell him about Ike and the snowmobile. We'll talk later."

After she and Sophie said good-bye, Liz's thoughts returned to Ike's second interview with Mrs. Otero. Ike was a skilled interrogator. If Mrs. Otero or Dolores had withheld any information during the first interview, she felt sure he could draw it out this time.

But what sort of information did he expect to get? She pictured Mrs. Otero hearing Ramon slip out of the apartment that night soon after she'd gone to bed. In her mind's eye, she saw Mrs. Otero getting out of bed and looking out the window to see where he was going. Would it have been too dark for her to make out any more than shadowy figures confronting Ramon, or had a streetlight enabled her to see their faces and witness the fight that had almost claimed his life?

The prompt arrival of police indicated that someone had called 911, and the lapse of time between the moment Ramon confronted his attacker and the moment the police arrived at the scene must have been very short. Could the person who put in the call have been Mrs. Otero?

Liz recalled Joe's saying that Mrs. Otero might not have talked freely during the first interview because she was afraid. Maybe she feared reprisals against Dolores. If so, could this mean she got a good look at the ringleader's face and would be able to identify him? But when Ramon regained consciousness, would he corroborate the identification, or would he too think of possible danger to Dolores?

The sound of her cell phone broke into these imaginings and speculations. It was Dan.

"Just checking on you, Lizzie. I trust you're okay."

"Thanks for calling, Dan. I'm fine. I'm down in the Moscarettis' apartment. They have a fireplace going. How are you and Edna doing?"

"Like everyone else, we're snowbound, but so far, not too bad, thanks to plenty of warm clothing." He laughed. "This is the only time I ever wished I'd spent the night in my office. That's what the people from last night's shift had to do. When I called them this morning, they reported that the generator's working one hundred percent."

"They'll stay warm, but what about food?"

"Fortunately, most of the night workers brown bag it. That should tide them over till they can get out."

Liz was about to tell him about Ike's braving the storm in a snowmobile, when Dan said he had some other calls to make. He double-checked that she had his cell phone number in case she needed to contact him.

Now, she began to wonder how long it would take Ike and

Lou to reach the Otero apartment. She checked her watch. It had been almost half an hour since they'd left.

To pass the time, she read yesterday's newspaper and scanned the weather forecast with a wry smile. *Tomorrow, mostly fair with seasonable temperatures early in the day. Increasing cloudiness and colder during the afternoon. Rain developing during the evening. Chance of snow, 40%.*

She'd just finished reading yesterday's coverage of the impending gang war when Ike phoned.

"We got here a few minutes ago," he said. "It wasn't bad. Like Lou said, the wind was at our backs."

"Thanks for letting me know you're there, safe and sound."

Because she knew he wanted to get right to the interview, she held back asking a lot of questions, but she was too curious about Mrs. Otero's reaction to this second visit not to ask just one.

"Was Mrs. Otero surprised to see you again?"

"Yes, she was, but we'd barely set foot in the door when she told us some good news. She called the hospital about half an hour ago. Ramon has regained consciousness."

Chapter Twenty-three

Ramon, conscious! Would he now be able to identify his assailants, especially the ringleader?

Before Liz could put her thought into words, Ike told her he'd give her the details when he got back to the Moscarettis'. "I'll call you when we're on our way back," he said.

More waiting and wondering, Liz thought as they clicked off.

At that moment Rosa's voice sounded from the kitchen. "Look out the window, dearie. I think the snow's getting lighter."

Joe's voice chimed in. "No doubt about it."

Liz sprang from the sofa and hurried to look outside. Her spirits bounded when she saw the buildings across the street, hidden since last night behind a thick curtain of falling snow, now looming through scattered flakes.

She felt a sense of jubilance. This was the beginning of the end of the unexpected storm's relentless grip on the city. Smiling, she went into the kitchen.

"You're right, it's letting up," she said.

Rosa, in the midst of putting together ingredients for their minestrone lunch, returned the smile, saying, "I must say, I'm relieved. Another few days of this, and even I'd start running out of food."

"I'm going out to see if I can locate Ike's car," Joe said. "I know about where he parked it. Maybe I can—"

Shooting him an irate look, Rosa interrupted. "You want to get a heart attack? Don't even think about digging that car out of the snow."

"When the plows come through, they'll only bury it again, anyway," Liz said.

Ike would have to stay another night in the Moscarettis' spare bedroom, she thought. That meant they'd have plenty of time together, but with the Moscarettis' always within earshot, he wouldn't talk freely about his interview with Mrs. Otero. If the power would only come on, her apartment might get warm enough for them to go up there. She was itching to hear what he'd found out. Had Ramon identified his assailants, especially the one who'd plunged the knife into his neck? Her mind pictured the mean eyes and scarred chin of Pepe Barboa.

Now she heard Joe grumbling, insisting he only wanted to dig far enough to identify the Taurus. "Then, when Ike comes back, he won't have to guess where it is, and it will be easier for him."

Rosa gave a grudging nod. "Well, all right, but if you get stuck in a snowdrift, don't expect me to haul you out."

Liz's cell phone sounded at that moment. What a blessing the devices had been during the storm, she thought. Without them, people might have been completely cut off from fellow residents and the rest of the world.

She checked the caller ID. It wasn't familiar, but the voice she heard a moment later was.

"Hello, Lizzie darlin'!"

"Pop! How did you get through? I figured all the circuits were jammed."

"They are, but we got through on a cell phone from a neighbor. How are you doing up there?"

"Fine. I'm with Rosa and Joe, and the snow's starting to let up."

"Good. Here's your mother. I'll come back on in a few minutes."

After she'd talked with Mom, Pop, ever the homicide detective, wanted to know how the Ruiz case was going.

"Will Ike have it wrapped up before you take off on your honeymoon?" he asked.

"He says there's a good chance he will."

After they said good-bye, Pop's question lingered in her mind. Ike didn't seem to be discouraged, but time was running out. Again, she told herself she should get used to the possibility of leaving for the Bahamas with Manuel's killer still on the loose.

But Ike must be counting heavily on further information from Mrs. Otero. That, plus whatever information detectives from the other squad got from Ramon and passed on to Ike, would certainly help. The thought cheered her.

Ike phoned again about an hour later, saying they'd left the Otero apartment, and he was calling from the snowmobile.

He reported they were on their way east, across town. "It's still bitter cold, but now that the snow's stopped and the wind's died down, we're starting to see signs of life. A few supers and porters are already out, clearing entrances to residences and businesses." He laughed. "We saw one apartment building where the entrance was blocked by a huge drift, and a guy was climbing out his window with a snow shovel."

He went on to say that he and Lou had contacted the station house and found out that plans for a citywide mobilization were under way.

"Police and fire departments are going to spearhead a block-by-block, door-to-door canvass and rescue mission, aided by members of other organizations and individual volunteers," he said. "It won't be long before people will be getting help if they need it."

"Are you and Lou going to be part of it?" Liz asked.

"No. When I asked how we would fit into this mobilization plan, I was told that our lieutenant phoned in instructions for homicide detectives to keep working on their cases."

In the job of catching killers, it was business as usual, Liz thought.

"Are the plows at work so emergency vehicles can get through?" she asked.

"Yeah. We're seeing some plows and all-terrain vehicles too. But there's no chance of our getting caught in a traffic jam, so we'll make it back to the Moscarettis' pretty soon."

Suddenly, his voice took on a note of urgency. "I'm signing off, Liz. We see a woman outside a town house who seems to need help. She's trying to get through a big drift blocking her door, and she's waving to us, like she's trying to flag us down. . . ."

Just before he hung up, Liz heard Lou Sanchez's voice in the background.

"She's pregnant!"

The words rang in Liz's ears. A pregnant woman wouldn't be out in a snowdrift, waving at the first vehicle she saw, unless she'd gone into labor. All NYPD cops knew the basics for delivering babies, and more than a few of them had put that knowledge to use. When Pop was a rookie, he'd delivered twins in a taxi.

Ike and Lou would get the woman back into her house. Her unheated house. Talk about bringing a newborn into the cold, cold world!

She didn't expect to hear from Ike again for quite a while. She was surprised when he called little more than an hour later. That was some speedy delivery, she thought.

"Sorry I had to ring off in a hurry. . . ." he began.

"I understand," she said. "I heard Lou say the woman was pregnant, and I assumed she was in labor."

"Yeah. She was. Good thing we came along when we did."

"Was it a boy or a girl?"

"We don't know."

"What!"

"She told us she'd just started labor, so we got her to St. Vincent's hospital. We made sure she was admitted and helped her get in touch with her husband. She said he was snowed in at work all night."

"Too bad you missed the rare experience of delivering a baby," Liz said.

He laughed. "Yeah, but riding a snowmobile with a pregnant woman on my lap wasn't an everyday experience, either!"

By the time Ike and Lou got back to the Moscarettis' house, a plow had made the street passable and piled up even more snow against all the parked cars. But thanks to Joe's digging in the area where he believed Ike's car was buried, the Taurus was identifiable from the sidewalk.

They all ate lunch in front of the fireplace. After a big bowl of Rosa's minestrone sprinkled with parmesan, and two chunks of Italian bread, Lou said he had to get going.

"I want to return the snowmobile," he said. "I'll pick up my skis at the garage and head for our neighborhood grocery store. It's probably open by now, and we need milk and some other items."

"With the snow stopped, people who live nearby will be able to get to the store," Rosa said. "I hope your grocery isn't sold out of milk before you get there. Maybe I'd better give you a quart, just in case."

Lou shook his head. "Thanks, Rosa, but I'm planning to ski from the garage to the grocery and head home from there. I couldn't handle a quart of milk while I'm on skis."

Joe had a solution. He delved into his trove of military equipment and came up with a large knapsack. Lou took off with not only the milk, but a loaf of bread, half a dozen eggs, and a jar of minestrone too. Soon after he left, Ike and Joe went outside to survey the Taurus.

Watching from the front window, Liz saw them talking to two teenaged boys, evidently brothers, who'd just finished clearing snow from the entrance to their neighboring brownstone. It looked as if Ike and Joe were making a deal with the boys to help dig the Taurus out. Sure enough, moments later Joe came back into the house for his snow shovel and a broom.

Casting a wary look at Rosa, Joe said the boys were going to help Ike with the shoveling, and he promised her he'd confine his activity to sweeping.

"We'll have Ike's car dug out and swept off before dinnertime," he announced. "Ike can spend another night here, and tomorrow there should be enough streets cleared so he can get to the station house and to his apartment."

Rosa glanced at Liz. "It'll be much too cold for you in your apartment tonight, dearie. I'll make up the couch for you and lend you a warm nightie. You'll be nice and cozy, sleeping next to the fire."

"Oh, thanks, Rosa." Liz hoped Rosa didn't notice her lack of enthusiasm. Appreciative as she felt, she couldn't suppress the question in her mind. When would Ike get a chance to tell her about his interview with Mrs. Otero?

Standing at the window, she watched Joe and Ike and the boys at work. The snow was heavy, and it was slow going. After half an hour or so, they all came inside for a break, reporting that it was very cold.

Rosa must have anticipated that. She had coffee and hot chocolate ready. While they were all gathered around the fireplace, drinking the warming beverages, Ike managed to get in a whisper to Liz.

"I know you want to hear what I found out today. I've thought of a way we can get some time alone."

Her heart bounded. "You have? How . . . ?

He took her hand and gave it a gentle squeeze. "You'll see."

Again, he and Joe and the boys went out and got to work on the snow surrounding the Taurus. Heartened but puzzled, again Liz watched from the window.

Joe and the boys were working on the side of the car next to the walk, and she noticed that Ike had made his way around to the rear. He seemed to be concentrating on clearing an area back there.

Gradually, the side of the Taurus next to the walk was cleared. When she saw Joe starting to sweep the remaining snow off the front door and window, it suddenly came to her what Ike had in mind.

"I'm not staying inside any longer, like some hothouse flower," she told Rosa. "I'm going upstairs for my parka and boots."

Chapter Twenty-four

When Liz made her way down the partially cleared steps and sidewalk to the Taurus, Ike, still working at the back of the car, waved to her and flashed a broad smile. Joe brandished his broom and said she was just in time to keep Ike company. He and the boys were going to take another break.

As Joe and the boys started for the house, Ike slogged through the deep drifts to the sidewalk and caught her up in a hug.

"So, you figured it out!"

"I did, and I hope Joe and the boys take a good, long break. Have you finished back there?"

"Yeah. The exhaust's all clear."

He opened the front door of the car and got in, then extended a hand to help her follow. She closed the door. He drew her into his arms.

"Welcome to my igloo," he said, after a lingering kiss.

She snuggled closer to him. "I can see where the Eskimos have it pretty cozy."

"It'll be even cozier when I get the heater going," he said, turning on the ignition. "Give it a few minutes to warm up."

"It doesn't have to be warm for you to start telling me what you found out today," she said.

"Okay," he replied. "First of all, the only information Mrs. Otero got from the hospital was that Ramon came to this morning, and he's lucid. I guess the detectives from the other squad got the word, and they'll get over there as soon as they can to question him."

Liz had been hoping to hear that Ramon had named Pepe

Barboa as his primary assailant. She held back a frustrated sigh and asked, "What else did you find out?"

"Do you recall that I told you I was curious about Mrs. Otero's speaking such good English?"

"Yes . . ." And she also recalled wondering why he was giving that so much thought.

"Well, when we questioned her about her family background, she was evasive at first, but I managed to get her talking. She told me she'd gone to school in New York from first grade on and graduated from high school here."

"That explains it. But why would she be reluctant to answer your questions?"

"Could be they were illegals. I didn't probe her about it. That's not my job. I think that's what got her trusting me, because pretty soon she started talking freely. Among other things, she told me that both her parents died within a few years after she got out of high school."

"Is that when she went back to Mexico?"

"No. First she got married here—to a construction worker who died only two years after the marriage. She went back to Mexico soon afterward—to be with relatives, she said."

Liz recalled Dolores' telling her that her parents had come to New York from Mexico when she and Ramon were little.

"So, she married again in Mexico, Ramon and Dolores were born there, and a few years later the family came to New York. And you think they're illegals, and that's why Mrs. Otero was reluctant to talk freely?"

"That could be the reason."

She cast him a quizzical look. "What's all this got to do with Manuel's murder?"

He gave a shrug. "I just had to find out how come Mrs. Otero speaks such good English."

Why would he and Lou ride a snowmobile in a raging blizzard for something so irrelevant to the case? Liz's intuition told her he had another angle he wasn't ready to divulge.

She thought of her imaginings concerning Mrs. Otero on the night of the attack on Ramon. "I've been wondering how the police got to the scene so quickly that the attackers didn't even have time to steal Ramon's wallet," she said. "Do you think Mrs. Otero might have heard Ramon leave the apartment and looked out the window and . . . ?"

"And called the police?" Ike nodded. "I had the same thought. I asked her about it, and Dolores too. Neither of them heard him go out. Someone in their building or one nearby must have put in the call. I'm sure the detectives in the other precinct have been working on it."

"I hope when they locate the caller, he tells them the attack took place right under a streetlight, and he's able to give them a good description of the attackers," Liz said. *Especially the ringleader. Had the person who'd called 911 been close enough to notice a scarred chin?*

A sudden flash of memory brought back a thought she'd had during the confrontation between Ramon and the Serps after Manuel's funeral. She'd wondered how the police had responded so quickly to a call from a passerby, and she'd wondered if Ramon could have put in the call himself before he got out of his car. She expressed the idea to Ike.

He nodded. "That would answer some questions, such as, why he was so bold—confronting Serps on their own turf, deliberately angering them by refusing to give up Dolores' pin."

He caught Liz up in a hug. "You figured it right. Having already put in the call, Ramon knew the police would show up at any minute. He wanted the cops to see the Serps running away from the scene. He wanted them to look guilty. And he could have had exactly the same motive the night of his attack. He put in the call to the police himself. Nice work, Redlocks."

She took a moment to bask in the warmth of his approval before expressing another thought. "Ramon must not have realized how many Serps were there to get him that night. He probably thought he could defend himself for a few minutes until the cops arrived."

"But he accomplished what he set out to do—he made the Serps look bad again," Ike replied.

"It's as if he wants the cops blaming the Serps for any trouble between gangs," Liz said.

"Good observation," Ike replied, looking thoughtful. "Now, let's see if we can get something on the radio." He started fiddling with the dials.

Moments later they were listening to the first news broadcast they'd heard since the night before. Hearing a full report on the blizzard made Liz feel that conditions were gradually returning to normal.

A weather forecast was given as well. Liz and Ike exchanged smiles when they heard that the wind in the coastal region had shifted, and tomorrow was expected to be fair and sunny, with rising temperatures.

At that moment they heard the crunch of wheels in the snow and the noise of engines. Seconds later came the sound of doors slamming shut and the ring of voices.

"Sounds like a canvass-and-rescue crew has arrived on this street," Ike said.

Peering through the lone clear window, they saw men with snow shovels heading for entrances still blocked by drifts. Behind some of those blocked entrances were residents—possibly alone, cold, hungry, and physically unable to shovel themselves out, Liz thought.

When she saw more canvassers delivering food and other items to needy householders, she realized how lucky she'd been all through this crisis. She'd been well fed, comfortable, and surrounded by people who cared about her. Suddenly she felt guilty.

"I feel as if I should be helping," she said.

"Me too," Ike replied. "But this is a well-organized operation. We'd only be in the way." He paused to give her a hug. "Besides, we're helping by trying to get a killer off the streets."

She gave him a regretful look. "I haven't been much help to you on this one."

"Oh, yes, you have! You found out that Manuel Ruiz had a girlfriend. That got us going in another direction."

It seemed to Liz that he'd been going in the direction of Mrs. Otero's fluent English rather than Dolores' romance with Manuel.

"Did Dolores say anything helpful?" she asked.

"No. She was very quiet. Other than saying she hadn't heard Ramon leave the apartment the night of the attack, she only spoke up when I was ready to leave. She said she hoped we'd catch whoever killed Manuel and whoever attacked her brother."

Just then they saw Joe and the boys coming out of the house, picking up shovels and the broom from the steps.

"They're all set for more digging around the Taurus," Ike said. "I'll get out there and join them. Why don't you stay here and listen to the radio? I'll come back when I need a break."

"All right." She wriggled out of the car to let him leave, climbing back in again as quickly as she could. It was very cold out there.

On the radio, an announcer was reporting on the citywide canvass-and-rescue operation. He described the operation as being spearheaded by New York's police officers and firefighters. Volunteers were going door-to-door to locate residents needing help. Food, blankets, flashlights, and other items were being delivered to those who said they could hold out until power was restored. Jeeps, Hummers, and ambulances were transporting others to generator-heated buildings and hospitals.

"Every block in every neighborhood is being covered," he stated. "Cops, firemen, Army Reserve units, the Red Cross, Curtis Sliwa's Guardian Angels, Boy Scouts, civic and church organizations, and individual volunteers are among those working to see New York through this crisis. There have also been reports of some street gangs joining in."

Street gangs! Even Liz's wildfire imagination could not picture the likes of Pepe Barboa showing any compassion for the blizzard's victims. Still, there might be some gang members who hadn't degenerated into total viciousness. Ramon, for example. According to Dolores, he'd been very good to her and their mother. That meant he had some kindness in his heart. Perhaps if he were not lying in a hospital with a punctured neck, he'd be out working with other volunteers.

Funny how things turned out, she thought. Yesterday, the city was worrying about a gang war. Today, the conflict between Serps and Zumas was deep-sixed by snow.

A tapping sound brought her out of her musing. Through a section of windshield, she saw Ike's smiling face. She smiled back. Apparently they were making good progress. She decided to see for herself.

When she climbed out, she saw that the hood of the car was free of snow. Ike was working on the rest of the windshield, while the boys were delving into drifts on the driver's side.

"It's beginning to look like a car!" she exclaimed, giving Ike a hug and waving at the others. "What can I do to help?"

Ike paused in his work, looking thoughtful. After a moment he gave a nod. "I know what you can do. Keep the motor running. After I finish with the windshield, and Joe has swept off the residue, you can turn on the wipers to clear the last of it. When the boys get working on the rear window, you can turn on the defrost to speed things along."

Liz was glad she'd be doing something, little as it seemed. As she turned to get back inside the car, she glanced down the street and noticed it was gradually coming to life. Residents, dug out by rescue workers, were venturing from doorways. Some were already out on the street, searching for their vehicles in the snowbanks, starting to wield shovels.

Watching from the car, Liz saw a few women emerging from houses with brooms, others with Thermoses of coffee for the shovelers. She heard neighbors calling to one another, exchanging jocular comments. From somewhere down the street, Frank Sinatra was belting out a song via a battery-powered radio. When she noticed two six-packs of beer and a bottle of wine chilling in a snowdrift, she decided the area had taken on the aspects of a block party.

By the time the Taurus was completely freed from its enormous snowbank, early-evening shadows had started to gather.

"This has been quite an experience," Liz said, when they all called it quits, and she, Joe, and Ike headed for the house. "I didn't know you had so many friendly neighbors, Joe."

Joe laughed. "To tell the truth, neither did I. There were folks out there I'd never even spoken to before. That's New York for you. People can live on the same street, even in the same apartment building, and never get acquainted. It takes something like this to bring us together."

Entering the house, they were greeted by a mouthwatering aroma and the sound of Rosa's voice from the kitchen.

"Dinner will be ready soon. I'm making Italian sausage raviolis and a nice big antipasto. And, Joe, I got a bottle of Riserva Barolo out for you to open. It'll warm you all up and give you an appetite too."

Breathing in the delectable smell of Rosa's cooking, Liz felt sure that nobody's appetite needed whetting.

Later, after a round of wine at the fireside, followed by dinner and more wine, Rosa ordered Liz and Ike to stay by the fire while she and Joe did the dishes.

"You've done enough work today," she said, going into the kitchen with Joe.

Liz looked at Ike with a shake of her head. "You've put in a long, hard day, and Joe did too, but I didn't do anything much. Joe should be the one relaxing by the fire with you—not me."

Smiling, he drew her close to him. "Much as I like Joe, you're the one I'd rather relax by the fire with."

She returned the smile. Even after a morning of snowmobiling around Manhattan and an afternoon of digging out his Taurus, he wasn't too tired to make her feel special!

"Thanks," she said, giving him a kiss. "You must be exhausted. I guess you won't have to be rocked to sleep tonight."

"Right," he replied. "No lying awake with the Ruiz case on my mind." He took a quaff of his coffee. "I should be hitting the sack soon. I have a full day tomorrow. I want to get going early."

She sensed that he wasn't ready to tell her how he was going to fill his day. She quelled her curiosity, along with the questions she would have asked. When he thought the time was right, he'd let her in on it. Maybe tomorrow.

Chapter Twenty-five

After her night on the Moscarettis' fireside couch, Liz awoke very early. She would have thought it was still the middle of the night if the fire hadn't already burned down to a few embers. She groped for the flashlight Rosa had given her and checked her watch. Five-thirty. Too early for anyone else to be up.

Suddenly, she realized the room felt warm, even though the fire had gone out hours ago. Had the power come back on during the night? Hopefully, she tried the lamp next to the couch. Instantly, the room filled with light.

Elated, she put on the robe Rosa had provided, thrust her feet into her heavy socks, grabbed her clothes, and headed for the door. Her apartment would be warm. She could take a hot shower in her own bathroom and get dressed in something that didn't make her look and feel like a refugee from Siberia.

The first thing she did after switching on her living room lights was turn the TV on. An early-morning news show was in progress. She gazed at the commentators, two men and a woman, noticing they all looked slightly disheveled, but—good for them—they'd made it to their jobs. She told herself she'd never take television for granted again.

She'd showered and almost finished dressing when her landline rang. Something else she'd never again take for granted.

Ike's voice came over the line. "Good morning!"

"Good morning. How did you know I was up here?"

"Early bird Lou called me on my cell and let me know the

power and phones are back on. I got up to tell you, and when you weren't on the couch, I figured it out."

"Are Rosa and Joe awake yet?"

"I don't think so. Everything's quiet."

"Come on up. I'll make coffee."

"Okay, give me a few minutes to shower, and I'll throw on my clothes and get up there on the double. But I'm warning you—with no shave since Sunday morning, I'm not looking like Prince Charming."

She held back the urge to inform him that he didn't have to look like Prince Charming to tell her what was going to keep him so busy all day.

Liz and Ike were enjoying their coffee, reveling in the warmth of the apartment and the miracle of TV. Liz was hoping Ike would let her in on his latest angle, when a knock sounded on the front door, followed by Joe's voice.

"Liz? Ike? We figured you were up here. Rosa says breakfast's almost ready."

Liz sprang to open the door. "Thanks, Joe. We'll be down in a few minutes. Isn't it wonderful to have power again?"

"Sure is. I just checked around outside. It's not so cold, and it looks as if we're going to get some sunshine. And a salt truck came through during the night, Ike, so the snow on the street is starting to melt."

"Good," Ike said. "That means I won't have trouble getting around."

Getting around where? Again, Liz wondered what was going to keep him occupied all day.

After Joe left, Ike looked at her with a slight frown. "I get the feeling you were hoping we'd have time to discuss the case."

She nodded. "Yes, I did. But we can do that tonight."

On their way to the door, he replied, "There's a chance I might be tied up tonight. I'll phone you later and let you know. But even if I can make it, don't count on anything new and exciting for us to discuss."

Although he softened the blunt statement by giving her a hug and a kiss, his words hammered her mind.

Did he mean he wasn't sure anything "new and exciting" would develop today, or was he saying that, even if it did, he wasn't going to tell her?

The question haunted her all through Rosa's pancake breakfast. It lingered after she stood at the Moscarettis' front window and watched Ike wave good-bye from the Taurus. She knew it would stay in her mind until she got some answers.

She was on her way upstairs, when she heard her landline ringing. It was Dan.

"Hello, Lizzie. Hope you weren't asleep and I'm not calling too early for you. Just checking on you and making sure you know the phones are working again and the power's on."

"Good morning, Dan. I've been up for a while. Looks as if everything's getting back to normal."

She was about to ask him if she should try to get into work, when he answered the question himself. "Better give it another day before coming to the office, Lizzie. The sidewalks aren't cleared, and I got word that the subways and busses aren't up to schedule yet. Engineers and drivers are having trouble getting to their jobs. I don't want you stuck somewhere."

"Okay, Dan," she said. "I'll see you tomorrow."

She turned the TV to a news channel for an update on the post-storm conditions. Shots taken all around Manhattan and other boroughs indicated that the city was struggling to get back on track. A few businesses had opened, but most were still closed. A Board of Education spokesperson announced that schools would remain closed until further notice.

Sophie phoned to report that she and Ralph were reporting for duty that day.

"We're not sure if the subways are back on schedule, so Ralph's going to walk to his station house, and I'm hitching a ride with a neighbor who works near mine," she said. "Are you going to work today? And how about Ike? Did he get his car dug out yet?"

Liz filled her in, adding, "He took off early this morning. I think he and Lou are on to something hot. He didn't say what. All he said was that he'd be very busy all day and maybe tonight too."

"It's not like Ike to hold back telling you *something,*" Sophie said.

"I know. It's bugging me."

"Maybe he and Lou are close to solving the case, and he wants to surprise you."

"I don't want to be surprised—I want to be in on it."

"Well, hang in there," Sophie said. "I gotta go. I'll call you tomorrow at work. Remember, we're going shopping for your bikini one night this week, as soon as the department stores are open."

Liz wasn't thinking of bikinis when she and Sophie clicked off. Was Sophie right? she asked herself. Was Ike withholding information from her because he was close to solving the case and wanted to surprise her with the good news?

Did he pick up on something in his second interview with Mrs. Otero that he hadn't told her? Or had something developed within the Ruiz family? For the first time in days, she thought about Carlos and Geraldo.

She recalled what Ike had said about Carlos' avoiding looking at Manuel's casket. Carlos must have been very angry with Manuel for the cruel words he'd spoken to the grandmother. Had Ike reconsidered ruling out Carlos' devotion to his mother as a motive for murder?

As for Geraldo, her previous thoughts about him as the possible killer were still strong in her mind. Had Ike's investigation turned up any evidence against Geraldo?

Or maybe he and Lou had checked with the hospital and found out that Ramon had identified Pepe Barboa as the assailant who'd stabbed him. Was Barboa now in custody at the other precinct? Would Ike be allowed to question him?

If anyone could worm the truth out of Barboa, it would be

Ike. Pop had told her Ike was exceptionally good at that. Given a chance to question Barboa, Ike would also have a good shot at getting a confession to Manuel Ruiz's murder.

For a few moments she felt as if she'd figured it all out. But when the moments passed, she knew she hadn't. Ike had known, days ago, that the scar-chinned Serp had a record for assault with a deadly weapon—a stiletto. If he'd suspected that this guy was the killer, wouldn't he have made him a "person of interest" and interviewed him right away?

There had to be another angle. Whether or not Ike was planning to surprise her with a wrap-up of the case, she had to be patient.

Chapter Twenty-six

Ike phoned later in the day to tell her he'd be tied up all that evening.

"By the time I'm through, it will be too late for me to come over," he said. "I'm sorry, Redlocks."

"Redlocks!" she exclaimed. "Sherlock wouldn't approve of your using that parody of his name if he knew how little I'm doing to help solve this case."

"I told you, you've been very helpful," he replied. "You got us headed in a new direction."

"Dolores and Manuel's romance? You would have found out about that eventually."

"Yeah, but you saved us a lot of time. If it hadn't been for your giving us that lead, we wouldn't be this far along on the case."

Abruptly, he changed the subject. "I'm glad you didn't try to get to work today."

"Me too. Dan called and said to wait until tomorrow."

"By tomorrow the subways and busses will be running on schedule, and general conditions will be much better."

She wanted to say she wished conditions with the case would be better, and he wouldn't be tied up every night, but she held off. That would be nagging him.

Perhaps he sensed her thought. "I'm sorry I've been so busy," he said. "And the bad news is, it'll probably continue all this week and into the next. I'll take a break to attend the bachelor party the squad's throwing for me on Saturday night, and of course I haven't forgotten our appointment with our two clergymen on Friday night. I'll make that, no matter what."

She knew he was telling her she wouldn't be seeing much of him this week or next.

When they said good-bye, she realized that if his sudden busy streak lasted through Sunday and the first of next week, they wouldn't see each other until the night of their rehearsal dinner. Starting next Wednesday, she was taking time off from work and going to stay with Gram until after the wedding.

Cheer up, she told herself. It had to mean that Sophie was right. Ike was putting in all his time making sure the case was wrapped up before they left on their honeymoon, and he was going to surprise her with the good news. But when did he plan to spring the surprise? Her wildfire imagination went into action. She pictured him whispering the name of the killer into her ear just after Pastor Drucker and Father Flynn pronounced them husband and wife.

Liz was at work the next day, when Sophie called from her squad car, saying the department stores were open and most sidewalks were clear. "Are you up for shopping tonight?" she asked. "We gotta get you a bikini."

Liz felt her spirits rise. At least this would be one night with no moping around her apartment, missing Ike. "You bet!" she replied. "A bikini's on my list, but Mom sent me some neat things from Florida, including a dress for dancing under the stars, she said. So I won't buy much. Besides, I'm saving up for Ike's wedding gift."

They met at five-thirty inside Macy's Herald Square entrance. It reminded Liz of their pre-Ike and Ralph days, when she and Sophie used to meet almost every day after work, sometimes to shop, sometimes just to have coffee somewhere, before heading home on the Staten Island ferry.

She bought white Bermuda shorts, two T-shirts—one yellow, one green—and white sandals. But she didn't find a bikini she would feel comfortable wearing.

"I want something more on me than a couple of handkerchiefs," she said.

"Yeah, they've gotten so skimpy, it's time they went out of style," Sophie replied. "Let's grab something to eat at a fast-food place and then check out the stores along Thirty-fourth Street and on Fifth Avenue."

In Lord and Taylor's, they both pounced on a turquoise bikini.

"Try it on," Sophie urged. "It looks like it has more yardage than the others we've seen."

It did. Liz imagined Ike giving her an admiring once-over as they strolled, hand in hand, on a Bahamas beach. The mental picture gave her a thrill of anticipation. She felt as if the days were not passing fast enough. She wanted the time to fly. But she also wanted Manuel's murder solved before her wedding day. Suddenly she felt an acute need for Ike to let her know where his investigation was going. Never mind the surprise.

"What else do you need?" Sophie asked, after Liz added the bikini to her purchases.

Before Liz could hold back the words, she found herself blurting, "I need Ike to tell me what's happening with the Ruiz case."

"Oh, Liz . . ." Sophie gave her a hug. "You know he's planning to tell you as soon as he's sure who the killer is. If he had any idea you felt so left out, he'd let you know what's going on. Maybe you should tell him."

Liz shook her head. "If he wants to surprise me, I don't want to nag him."

"So, let him surprise you. You should be thinking about your wedding, not fretting about this," Sophie said. "Have you decided what you're going to give Ike for a wedding present? You should be doing something about that pretty soon."

Liz brightened. "Yes, I've thought about Ike's present, but so far I haven't come up with anything that rings the bell. I want it to be something he'll really go for."

"Let's browse in some other stores," Sophie said. "Maybe you'll find something tonight."

They looked at watches and luggage and handsome designer shirts with monograms included in the hefty price. A sterling silver hairbrush also caught Liz's eye. She could picture Ike running it over his tousled blond thatch. Top grain leather driving gloves would be good too, she thought. She'd noticed that Ike's gloves were getting shabby, and, besides, they were what the stores called *faux leather.* Still, nothing seemed special enough.

"I don't see anything that says, 'This is it'," she told Sophie. "But with Ike on the case every night, I'll have plenty of free time after work to look around some more."

Later, at home, Liz made coffee and sat down on the living room sofa to watch TV. After catching the news and getting only a rehash on the Ruiz case, she turned to the movie channel, where an old black-and-white World War II film, starring Gregory Peck as an Army Air Corps pilot, was starting.

Ike liked World War II movies, and he'd especially like this one, she thought. Even on her dinky little set, it looked good. When they got around to buying a new TV with the oversized screen he wanted, plus all the bells and whistles, she'd get this film for him in a video store. He'd love watching movies on a big screen. She remembered his saying it would be like being in a theater.

In a flash, it came to her. *My wedding gift to him will be a TV with the biggest screen available!*

They'd discussed it often enough that she knew exactly what to get. Sure, it would be expensive, but knowing Ike would flip over it, she didn't care. She'd put it on her credit card and pay it off in two or three months. She'd buy it over the weekend and enlist Joe's help in installing it.

With Ike working the first part of the week, and her in Staten Island from Wednesday on, it looked as if he wouldn't see his dream TV until they returned from their honeymoon.

Meanwhile, at the rehearsal dinner, she'd give him something small he'd think was his gift.

She found herself laughing. He wasn't the only one who'd be springing a surprise!

Chapter Twenty-seven

Liz's excitement over getting Ike the big-screen TV she knew he wanted overcame her feeling of being excluded from his case. On Thursday evening she consulted with Joe, and he said he'd go with her on Saturday to help select it and arrange for delivery. Over and over she visualized Ike's delight when they returned from their honeymoon and he discovered his dream TV in place of her thirteen-incher. She smiled every time she thought about it.

Ike must have noticed her upbeat mood when he came to pick her up for their meeting with the clergymen on Friday night.

"You're all smiles tonight," he said on their way to Pastor Drucker's rectory.

"That's because we're together for the first time since Tuesday morning," she replied. *That's part of it anyway.*

She didn't need to remind him that this would probably be the last time they'd see each other until their rehearsal dinner the next Friday night. His next comment told her he was well aware of it.

"This has been one hell of a week for us," he said. "And it looks as if it won't get any better for a few more days. You're heading for Gram's on Wednesday, right?"

"Right." Was he saying there was a chance the case would be sewn up by Wednesday?

Evidently not. "I wish I could promise you some good news before you go over to Staten Island," he said.

She laughed. "Just as long as you give me the good news before we're standing at the altar."

"You can count on that," he replied.

He must be very close to a wrap-up, she thought.

The meeting with the two clergymen went very well. Liz had known Father Flynn since she was in grade school, but she'd never met Pastor Drucker. Ike had met Father Flynn at Sophie and Ralph's wedding, and he'd recently become acquainted with the Lutheran pastor.

By the time the meeting ended, Liz felt almost as much at ease with the Lutheran minister as she was with her Catholic priest. She was confident that the ecumenical ceremony would please Pop, Mom, and Gram, and Ike's parents and his great-aunt Hilda too.

Driving back to the apartment, she cast him a teasing look, saying, "Well, you've just taken another giant step away from bachelorhood."

He took a hand off the wheel long enough to give hers a gentle squeeze. "I wish I'd just taken the *final* step," he replied.

In the apartment, he settled himself on the sofa while she made coffee.

"This seems like the good old days," she said, bringing their mugs from the kitchen.

"We'll soon be back there, only it will be even better," he replied. "The Ruiz murder case will be history, we'll be married, and . . ." He paused, glancing at her TV. ". . . and maybe, before long, we'll have one of those big screens."

"You'd really like that, wouldn't you?" she asked, trying to keep a straight face.

"Yeah, it'd be great for watching sports events and movies. You want to get one too, don't you?"

"Yes, I'd love one."

"Then what are we waiting for? I know they're expensive, but we don't spend money on Broadway shows and fancy restaurants. Let's plan on buying one as soon as we get back from our honeymoon."

"Okay," she said, trying to keep her smile from escalating

into a laugh that might have made him wonder what was so funny.

The next afternoon, Liz and Joe went to one of the large appliance stores, and she bought an oversized-screen TV that Joe assured her any man would love. They arranged for delivery on Monday. Joe said he'd hook it up while she was at work. Later, a phone call from Ike, just to say good night, ended another day.

On Sunday, in anticipation of the oversized TV, she moved her little set into the bedroom. By the time she got home from work on Monday, Ike's dream TV had been delivered, and Joe had it hooked up.

She gazed at it, almost in awe, wishing that Ike didn't have to wait so long to see it. When he phoned later that evening, she was tempted to tell him she had a surprise for him and ask him if he could possibly spare a little time to drop by. But before she gave in to the temptation, he told her he was in his apartment, on the Internet, and he had to say good-bye and get back to work.

Tuesday. Her last day at work before leaving for Staten Island and a flurry of last-minute wedding details. Pop and Mom and also Ike's family were due to arrive on Thursday. And on Friday night she'd see Ike again. She remembered his promise. She could count on the case being solved before the wedding. They'd enjoy their honeymoon without wondering who'd plunged a stiletto into Manuel Ruiz's throat and left him to die.

That night she packed her luggage with the clothes she'd be wearing in the Bahamas, plus enough to wear until Saturday. She planned to take a taxi to the ferry, and Gram was going to pick her up in St. George.

Watching the late news on the big screen, she realized that Ike hadn't phoned to say good night. Was he on the Internet again? What was he looking for online?

Those questions gave rise to another. Had Ramon named his assailant? There'd been nothing about it on the news.

She was just about to turn off the television and get ready for bed, when her intercom buzzer sounded. Who would be coming to her place at that hour? she wondered. She went to answer it.

Ike's voice sent quivers of joy into her heart. "Buzz me in, Redlocks!"

Moments later he was in the apartment, and she was in his arms, forgetting everything except that he was there. By the time her senses settled down, she heard him utter something, somewhere between a gasp and a grunt. She knew he'd noticed the big TV. It would have been hard not to.

"Surprise!" she said. "It's your wedding present, from me."

He stared at her, then back at the TV. "You . . . you got this for me, all by yourself?"

"Joe helped me pick it out, and he set it up. Do you like it?"

Recovered from his surprise, he picked her up and swung her around, saying, "Like it? It's exactly what I wanted! Thank you!"

After a kiss and a hug, he went for a closer look, visually measuring the size of the screen, examining the buttons, and studying the remote before turning it on. A commercial was in progress. He watched it, looking spellbound.

"I'll make coffee," she said.

He nodded, muttering, "I can't get over the size of this baby."

When she came back with their mugs, he had the movie channel on. Ginger Rogers, in a swirly gown, and Fred Astaire in white tie and tailcoat, were prancing over chairs and tables. Although Liz knew he'd much prefer a World War II battle scene, he seemed fascinated.

When she set the mugs on the coffee table, he looked up and turned off Ginger and Fred. Reaching for her hands, he drew her down beside him.

"I'm still overwhelmed, Liz. Did I say thanks?"

She laughed. "Yes, you did."

"Well, thanks again. This was one of the best surprises of my life."

"I didn't expect you to see it until we got back from the Bahamas," she said. "And I didn't think *I'd* see *you* until Friday night, Having you drop in tonight was a nice, big surprise for *me* too."

With a broad grin, he put on an old-movie, tough-guy accent, reminiscent of Humphrey Bogart.

"Shweetheart, from surprises, you ain't heard nothin' yet!"

Chapter Twenty-eight

Liz stared at Ike. Had he found out who killed Manuel Ruiz? Or did he mean there'd been a surprising development in the case, and he was going to let her in on it?

He looked at her with a smile. "I know I haven't been very communicative lately," he began.

"Well, that's an understatement if ever I heard one!" she exclaimed.

"Don't get your Irish up. I had a good reason. And, like I said, you're in for a big surprise."

She got the feeling he was teasing her. "If you're going to enlighten me at last, I'd rather you got right to it and skip the 'good reason,' " she said.

He hesitated, looking uncertain. "I wanted to . . . well, okay, I guess it can wait till after I fill you in. I'll start with Mrs. Otero. I know you were puzzled about my interest in her."

She nodded. "You told me you were curious about her fluent English, but I felt sure there had to be another angle."

"There was. Call it a hunch, but I had a strong feeling that what she told me about going back to Mexico after her first husband died, and remarrying and having the two kids there, wasn't one hundred percent accurate. Then I remembered something you said, and it got me thinking."

"Something I said?" She looked at him in puzzlement.

"Yeah. Lou and I had been following a lead about a violent incident in Carlos Ruiz's past, but after I told Lou what you'd said, we decided to hold off investigating Carlos and do some research on Mrs. Otero."

More about Mrs. Otero? By now Liz had grown impatient. "Wait a minute," she broke in. "What *about* the remark I made?"

"I'll get to that," he replied. "Hear me out. In my first interview with Mrs. Otero, she told me the name of the Manhattan high school she'd attended, and when Lou and I interviewed her together, she mentioned her first name—Ana Luisa. We'd succeeded in getting her to open up to us, and we didn't want to turn her off by asking what her maiden name was, but by estimating her age, we guessed at the year she might have graduated from high school. A little digging through school records and yearbooks, and we found Ana Luisa Morales. She still looks like her yearbook picture. After that, we tackled the Bureau of Vital Statistics, starting with the marriage records."

What link could Mrs. Otero's statistical background possibly have with Manuel Ruiz's murder? That question temporarily drove the matter of her own chance remark into the back of Liz's mind. Without interruption, she listened to what else Ike had to say.

"We found the record of a marriage between Ana Luisa Morales and a Conrad Davis," he continued. We figured he must have died, and we verified that in the death records. Next, we looked up their birth records. Both she and Davis were born in New York."

Mrs. Otero, a U.S. citizen? If this was the surprise he'd mentioned, it fell short of her expectations, Liz thought. Still, it was an interesting angle.

"I didn't have the slightest inkling that Mrs. Otero was born here," she said. "I thought she was brought here from Mexico when she was a child. I guess I got that impression from Dolores."

"I had that impression too, at first," Ike replied. "But that's not all we dug up. While we were in the birth files, Lou found the record of a daughter born to Ana Luisa and Conrad Davis." He paused to look into Liz's eyes before adding, "The child's name was Dolores."

This must be the surprise. Stunned, Liz attempted to put it all together.

"Dolores! She was a baby when her mother took her to Mexico after the first husband died. *He* was Dolores' father, not the second husband."

Ike nodded. "Right."

Why had Mrs. Otero let Ike believe that Juan Otero was the father of Dolores, and that she had been born in Mexico? Liz wondered.

Ike seemed in no hurry to enlighten her. She got the feeling that he was feeding her bits and pieces of information and waiting to see if she could put them together. But, surprising as this new development about Mrs. Otero was, it seemed irrelevant to Manuel's murder.

Ike must have sensed her annoyance. "Sorry," he said. "I get a kick out of watching you try to figure things out. Give you a little time, and you're on to it."

"I'm delighted to be a source of amusement," she replied. She knew her voice had a decided edge to it, but for days she'd been patient, waiting for him to tell her how things were developing, and now he was playing games.

"It's not amusement, it's amazement," he said. "I never cease to be amazed at the way that steel-trap mind of yours snaps up clues."

Somewhat mollified, she flashed him a smile. "Thanks. But how about giving me some real bait? What's going on with Ramon? Has he named Pepe Barboa as the one who stabbed him?"

"I was getting around to that," he replied. "But I haven't finished telling you about Mrs. Otero yet."

"I'm more interested in what's going on with Pepe Barboa and Ramon," she replied.

"Okay, I'll get back to Mrs. Otero later. About Barboa. The other precinct has him in custody. I was in on the questioning today."

"And . . . ?"

"He admits he stabbed Ramon but claims it was self-defense. A slick attorney was there during the questioning. Looks as if he's going to get Barboa off with a light sentence, if any."

"And he can't be charged with suspicion of Manuel's murder?"

"There's no evidence connecting him to it in any way."

So that angle was a dead end, she thought. But he'd mentioned he and Lou had been investigating a violent incident in Carlos Ruiz's past, and she'd assumed Geraldo was also still a person of interest.

"What about Uncle Carlos and Geraldo? Anything new about them?" she asked.

"No. They're both out of the picture now," he replied.

That meant someone else was *in* the picture. Ike was still enjoying himself, giving her scraps of information. A sudden thought struck her. What if he hadn't dropped in tonight just to bring her up to date on the case? Maybe he was having a little fun before letting her know he'd found out who killed Manuel. The more she considered it, the stronger the possibility became, until she felt sure that was exactly what he'd been doing.

Now she was determined to figure everything out for herself, before he decided it was time to tell her. Let him have his fun! This had turned into sort of a contest. She started reviewing what he'd told her that night and putting it together with what she already knew.

"You're quiet all of a sudden," he said.

She needed more time. "Let's take a break from the case and watch a movie on your dream TV," she replied.

A slight frown crossed his face. It vanished as he glanced toward the big screen. "I wanted to get around to that other matter I mentioned before, but okay."

Translation: He's enjoying himself, having a little fun with me until he's ready to spring the ultimate surprise, but he's also eager to watch a movie on the big screen.

And so that "other matter" might be the name of Manuel's killer, she thought. He'd let her know when he was ready.

But she wanted to do some heavy concentrating on what he'd told her and beat him to it.

"You can get around to the 'other matter' after the movie's over," she said. That would give her plenty of time to figure it out.

Fortunately, a war movie titled *Hellcats of the Navy* was just starting. Just as she'd planned, after making numerous favorable comments about the giant screen, Ike settled into watching the film.

She closed her eyes. Shutting everything else out of her mind, she concentrated on what he'd just told her. Although she had previously thought that the information about Mrs. Otero's second marriage in Mexico didn't have anything to do with the case, now she reviewed it very carefully.

A few moments later, like a bolt of lightning, the truth struck her mind, bringing everything into sharp focus. Her belief that Mrs. Otero's background was irrelevant to Manuel's murder had overshadowed something obvious—something she should have seen the instant Ike told her about Dolores' being born in New York.

Mrs. Otero, then Mrs. Davis, had gone back to Mexico with her baby after the death of her first husband. There she met and married a Mexican man named Otero. But the fact that Dolores had not been born of that marriage provided another startling reality.

If Mrs. Otero had given birth to Ramon, he would be younger than Dolores—not older!

Now the whole truth struck her. Mrs. Otero's second husband had likely been a widower raising a young son. *Ramon and Dolores are not brother and sister!*

Liz didn't take time trying to figure out why Mrs. Otero had given Ike and everyone else an untruthful impression. Her mind had already recalled an idea she'd had after the incident following Manuel's funeral, when she and Dolores had been accosted by the Serps who wanted Dolores' pin.

Ramon Otero had arrived at the scene, demanding that they let go of his sister. She remembered his frank affection for Dolores, how extremely protective he was of her, and, later, in the car, how obvious was his hatred of her Serp boyfriend. But, most of all, she remembered the question that sprang into her mind. *Could Ramon's overprotectiveness of Dolores have led him to murder Manuel?*

When she'd questioned Ike about the possibility, his reaction at the time had been negative. "I can see where he'd be angry about his sister dating a Serp, but I can't picture him flying into a homicidal rage over it," he'd said. He'd gone on to say that, in his experience, emotions such as familial devotion and protectiveness didn't ignite the urge to kill.

But he'd also mentioned that extreme jealousy of a spouse or paramour often did. Newspaper headlines and TV bulletins were proof of that.

If Ramon knew he wasn't Dolores' brother, what if he'd fallen in love with her? Finding out she was in love with someone else, especially a detested Serp, would have stirred up both rage and jealousy—a deadly combination of emotions.

Suddenly, she knew this wasn't supposition. It was true. And she had no doubt that Ike too now knew the truth. He'd been waiting to see how soon she'd catch on.

She glanced at Ike, absorbed in the movie, evidently completely unaware that she'd been trying to figure things out for herself. She wanted to let him know she'd picked up the clue he'd dropped, about Dolores' being born in New York, and taken it to its conclusion.

Just then, Ike turned his head and noticed her looking at him.

"What?" he asked, but his eyes were already glancing back at the screen, where Navy pilot Ronald Reagan was engaged in aerial combat over the Pacific.

She knew she had to say something startling to compete with a war movie on an oversized screen.

"Ramon's the killer," she replied.

Chapter Twenty-nine

Ike turned off the TV and drew her into a hug. "You got it, Redlocks! I knew you would!"

They paused for a kiss, during which Liz realized they hadn't done any serious kissing since Friday night.

The same thought must have occurred to Ike. When the kiss ended, he looked into her eyes, saying they'd never have to go through a spell like that again.

"By the time I'm on my next homicide, we'll be married. I'll have you and my computer right here within arm's reach."

"And when I'm not in your arms, I can sneak a few peeks over your shoulder while you're digging for information online," she said. "Your days of keeping me in the dark are numbered."

"I admit I clammed up on you about what I was looking for online," he replied. "I believed we were close to wrapping up the case, but I wanted to be one hundred percent sure before I told you. I didn't want to build you up for a letdown.

"I understand now," she said, giving him a kiss.

He smiled. "Good. I have much more to tell you, but before we get into the case again, there's that matter I mentioned before. . . ."

She broke in. "Before we get to that, I have a question. You told me I said something that led you to look into Mrs. Otero's statistical background. What did I say?"

"I want to get to that other matter first," he replied.

"Can't it wait?" she asked. "I'm really curious to know what I possibly could have said that made you suspect Ramon."

"Well . . . okay. Remember when you asked me if I thought Ramon could be the killer?"

"Sure. And you said you'd never seen family devotion ignite the urge to kill, like jealousy of a spouse or lover often did."

"Yeah, but then you said it was a good thing Ramon was Dolores' brother, because I already had more than enough suspects to investigate."

So that was it! She stared at him with a big smile. "One little remark got you thinking that Ramon might *not* be Dolores' brother!"

"Right. The first seed of suspicion was sown. After our research told us Dolores was born here, we knew we were on to something, but we had to nail it down. Through the Internet, I was able to contact the Bureau of Vital Statistics in Hermosillo, the Mexican city Mrs. Otero told me they came from. It's a good-sized city that became somewhat Americanized after Ford Motors built a plant there several years ago. Although most of our contacts were able to respond in English, Lou's fluency in Spanish got us what we were looking for without delay."

"So you found out that Ramon's mother wasn't Ana Luisa Otero?"

He gave an impatient nod. "Yeah, we did, but let's sidetrack for a few minutes. I want to attend to that matter I mentioned before."

Much as Liz wanted to continue discussing this surprising development, she sensed Ike's urgent need to switch topics. Whatever it was, it must be important to him. "Okay, go ahead," she said.

"Wrapping up the Ruiz case wasn't the only reason I've been so busy," he replied. Reaching into his pocket, he brought out a small box. "It took some time to find exactly what I wanted to give you for a wedding present, but here it is."

He opened the box, and she gazed in delight at a sapphire pendant in a platinum setting. She expressed her heartfelt thanks with a kiss.

"I love it!" she exclaimed. "I love *you!*"

"Sapphire's your birthstone," he said. "And our names are engraved on the back, with our wedding date."

She took the pendant out of the box and smiled at the inscription. He fastened the chain around her neck. She kissed him again.

"The way I kept putting you off just now, it's a wonder you didn't change your mind about giving it to me," she said.

He laughed. "I wanted to give it to you tonight, but I'd almost decided to wait until Saturday. I thought you were never going to let me get around to it."

"I'm glad I finally shut up. This date will always be special for us. We'll always remember giving each other our wedding gifts."

"It will also be special as the night we both knew we wouldn't have to go on our honeymoon with Manuel's killer still at large," he said. "And you figured it out before I got around to telling you."

"It was a good guess. Tell me more about how you put it together."

"Our first evidence was finding out that Ramon was born to a Carmella and Juan Otero," he replied. "The Hermosillo authorities are sending us a copy of his birth certificate. We also accessed the death records. Ramon's mother died two years after his birth."

"Why did Mrs. Otero want everyone to think Ramon was her son?" Liz asked. "Was it because Ramon was in this country illegally, and she believed her American citizenship would protect him from the INS?"

"Yeah, something like that." The expression on Ike's face suggested that he was about to make another startling revelation. What else could he possibly have unraveled in the tangled life of Mrs. Otero?

"There was no record of a marriage between an Ana Luisa Davis and a Juan Otero," he announced.

Liz stared at him in disbelief. "Could they have been married in some other city?" she asked.

He shook his head. "Lou looked into that. They lived together as a family, and she took his name, but evidently they never made it legal."

Liz turned the surprising statement over in her mind. She visualized Dolores' mother meeting Ramon's father after she went to Mexico with her baby. Had they fallen in love? Perhaps. But instead of marrying, they'd chosen to live together with their children, as a family. *Why didn't they marry?*

Ike answered the question before she put it into words. "The way we figure it, she went to Mexico planning to return to the U.S. before Dolores was ready for school. She wanted Dolores to be educated here. She didn't marry Otero because she thought that marrying a Mexican would jeopardize her citizenship and her child's. Seems she's slightly paranoid about how Immigration and Naturalization operates."

Liz shook her head, saying, "All this is mind-boggling. Hold that thought while I get refills on our coffee."

In the kitchen, her imagination went into action. Ramon's father must have wanted Ramon to be educated in the U.S. too. When they decided the time had come to go to New York, Dolores' mother brought Ramon and his father into the country illegally. How had she accomplished it? Liz could only guess. She pictured them crossing the border in a car purchased in Hermosillo by American citizen Ana Luisa Davis. She would have been at the wheel so that her fluent English would help get them in without a hassle. They could have passed as a Mexican American family returning from a visit with relatives.

Going back to Ike and handing him his coffee mug, she said, "So, Ramon knew from the start that he and Dolores weren't brother and sister."

Ike nodded. "Sure, he did. He had to be about four or five years old when Dolores and her mother came into the picture. Before that, his father would have told him that his mother had died."

Mrs. Otero—or, as Liz thought of her now, Dolores'

mother—had probably warned Ramon about the INS early on. She'd brought him into the country illegally, and, fearing reprisals, they'd kept the secret of his real mother between them. After he joined the Zumas, rumored to be involved in drug trafficking, his fear of the INS would have made him extra careful to keep the secret. And of course Dolores had been too young to remember when she and her mother went to live with Ramon and his father. She'd grown up believing that Juan Otero was her father, and Ramon her brother.

Recalling her ride in the backseat of Ramon's Mercedes, Liz reviewed the thoughts she'd had about him. Besides remembering how devoted to and overly protective of Dolores he'd seemed, she also recalled his hateful words about Manuel, and she'd been struck with the possibility that Ramon might be the killer. But with Ramon a protective brother instead of a jealous lover, the idea hadn't jelled.

"Detective Eichle, you're so smart to have figured out that Ramon and Dolores weren't brother and sister and to realize that he could have fallen in love with her and killed Manuel in a jealous rage," she said.

"We might not have gotten to the bottom of it without your help, Redlocks," he replied. "That remark you made pointed me in the right direction. After that it wasn't hard to figure out why Ramon was trying so hard to put the Serps into an especially bad light with the police. He was setting them up as Manuel's killers, with Pepe Barboa as the instigator."

"So Ramon is now under arrest, in the hospital?"

"Right. The other precinct turned him over to us. But of course before we arrested him for murder, we needed more than knowing he's not Dolores' brother. We had to get additional evidence."

Liz's mind went back to the police lab's exhaustive efforts to identify a set of unclear fingerprints on Manuel Ruiz's birthday card. At that time Ramon had not been a person of interest. He'd never been arrested, so his prints had not been on record. Now, they were. Did his prints have that distinctive whorl? Had the lab succeeded in matching them with the partial prints on the birthday card? Was this the additional evidence Ike had needed?

Close on this speculation came another. Had Ike and Lou found a stiletto in Ramon's apartment that tested positive for Manuel's blood?

She noticed Ike looking at her with a twinkle in his eyes. "Are you watching me 'trying to figure things out with my steel-trap mind?' " she asked with a wry smile.

"Yeah. Have you latched on to the additional evidence we got?"

"I was thinking Ramon's prints might have shown up on the birthday card, or maybe you found the murder weapon in his apartment."

"Zilch on the murder weapon. We figure the stiletto ended up in a sewer right after the murder, but you're close on the fingerprint angle. When the other precinct turned Ramon over to us, they also turned over his wallet," Ike began.

Liz gave an impatient shrug. Ramon's prints would be on his wallet and everything in it.

"There were several new large-denomination bills in the wallet," Ike went on. "We got a pretty good set of Ramon's prints from one particular bill. They showed a distinctive whorl."

Liz looked at him with a bewildered frown. Like all the bills in the wallet, of course that one would also have Ramon's prints on it. Besides, hadn't Ike told her that partial prints alone wouldn't stand up as evidence?

Ike's voice came into her thoughts. "That particular bill was a crisp, new C-note," he said.

Liz felt a rush of excitement. "Manuel's birthday money!" she exclaimed. "Manuel's prints were on it too! That's how you—"

With a shake of his head, Ike broke in. "Evidently Manuel never handled the bill. Never took it out of the card. His prints weren't on it."

Her excitement ebbed. Without Manuel's prints, Ramon's

prints on the bill would not prove it was the one stolen from the birthday card. One of his drug customers could have paid him with a new hundred-dollar bill. This wasn't irrefutable evidence.

She was about to express her disappointment, when Ike restored her previous elation with a clarifying statement. "But, in addition to Ramon's prints and an unidentified partial, most likely a bank teller's, we also lifted a beautiful set belonging to Gina Ruiz."

Chapter Thirty

On the palm-shadowed terrace of the hotel's beachfront café, Liz finished her lunch and let her gaze wander over the sandy shore and the sparkling expanse of water to the blended blues of the sea and sky.

She looked across the table at Ike. Their glances met in a mutual smile.

"Our last day in the Bahamas," he said. "And every one of them has been perfect."

"It's even more beautiful here than I imagined," she replied.

He reached for her hand, saying, "I was just thinking the same thing about you."

She leaned over and kissed him. Ike had barely set foot off the plane when he'd started coming up with romantic remarks quite unlike his usual bantering compliments. Now, with only four hours left until they boarded the plane for home, the *bon mots* were still flowing. She didn't know if it was the spell of the Bahamas or maybe just having his mind off homicides; she only knew she loved it.

"Your eyes are exactly the same color as the sea and sky," he continued. "And so's your bikini. Did you know that when you bought it?"

"Actually, I didn't think you'd even notice my eyes," she replied with a teasing smile.

He laughed and picked up their camera from the table. "Let's take one last walk along the beach. I want to get some more shots of you, eyes and all."

Watching her put on the wide-brimmed straw hat she'd

bought from a village vendor, he added, "And I want to get at least one shot without the hat, Redlocks."

"You haven't called me Redlocks since the night you came to tell me who murdered Manuel Ruiz," she said, as they walked, hand in hand, to the water's edge.

"Haven't I?" He gave her hand a squeeze. "With all the help you gave us on the case, I should have mentioned it during our marriage vows, but I wasn't thinking about the case at the time."

She laughed. "I guess it's been a while since either of us thought about it. Funny, how a murder mystery can take over your mind and almost dominate your life, and then suddenly—*poof*—it's gone."

He cast her a grin. "When did that *poof* happen for you? Was it when I told you Gina Ruiz's fingerprints were on that new bill in Ramon's wallet?"

"Well, Gina's prints on the bill left no doubt that it was the one stolen from Manuel's birthday card, and I got a wonderful feeling, knowing we didn't have to leave on our honeymoon with the case unsolved. But the real *poof* came when Pop was walking me down the church aisle, and I saw you waiting for me. At that moment any thoughts of Manuel Ruiz's murder just vanished from my mind."

"I know what you mean. When I saw you coming down the aisle, I felt my heart stand still for a second. All I could think of was, we were getting married, and I could hardly wait till you were my wife."

They smiled into each other's eyes.

"The night you came to tell me who murdered Manuel, you didn't tell me what other evidence you got to wrap up the case," she said.

He laughed. "As I recall, we got sidetracked."

She joined in the laugh. "And after that night we were so caught up in the wedding festivities, we didn't have a chance to discuss it," she said. "Do you realize we haven't talked about the case since that night?"

"Yeah. It's not what you'd call a honeymoon topic of conversation."

"It was the last thing on *my* mind too." She paused, reflecting. "For a while, Ramon had everyone fooled, didn't he?"

"Yeah, he was clever, throwing Manuel's wallet into the trash bin with nothing stolen from it. That eliminated robbery as a motive. And tossing Manuel's gang jacket into the trash too was part of the setup. It suggested that the Serps were involved and this was their way of disowning Manuel as a member. It might have worked if Ramon hadn't taken that bill from the birthday card."

"Now that we're back to talking about the case, there's something I need to ask you," Liz said.

"Something that needs clearing up?"

"Yes. After Ramon stabbed Manuel, he went through his pockets and found the birthday card, so his hands must have been bloody. . . ."

"And you're wondering why I didn't mention bloody prints on the card and the bill? There were no bloody prints. We figure Ramon wore gloves during the stabbing and took them off before he went through Manuel's pockets."

"And got rid of the gloves along with the murder weapon?"

"Right. He was very clever, up to a point."

"The point being his inability to resist stealing that crisp, new, one-hundred-dollar bill. That solved the case, didn't it?"

"As far as we were concerned, it did, but we didn't want to stop there. The more evidence we could get, the stronger the case would be. First, we started working on the motive. We figured it this way. When Ramon found out about the romance, he was jealous, but he believed that when the Serps ordered Manuel to break up with Dolores, that would be the end of it."

"But when the Serps found out they were still meeting secretly, and they told Ramon, he flew into an uncontrollable rage?"

"Yeah. That must have been what pushed him over the

edge. We figured that when Manuel returned to his home that night to put on the sweater and make peace with his grandmother, Ramon had just been told of the secret meetings. Furious, he jumped into his car and headed for the area where Manuel lived, planning to wait and waylay him on his way home from the meeting with Dolores. He didn't know that Manuel had come home to put on the sweater and apologize to his grandmother."

"Ramon drove his Mercedes with that Montezuma logo on the back into Serps territory?" Liz asked in surprise.

"Well, we felt sure he wouldn't have gone there on foot. Yeah, he was taking a chance. He must have been out of his mind with jealousy. We believe that when he saw Manuel leave the house to go back to Dolores, he tailed him and planned to attack him later, when he was on his way home."

"Why would he wait? How come he didn't attack Manuel on his way to Dolores? You'd think he'd want to keep them from having one last tryst."

"Yeah, but when Manuel left the house the second time, it was still early in the evening. Too many people around. Most likely Ramon decided that by the time Manuel was on his way home, it would be late, and the streets in that area would be deserted."

"I get it," Liz said. "Ramon probably found a parking spot near that delicatessen alley and waited for the deli to close. Then he stashed the Mercedes in the alley and waited for Manuel to pass by."

"Yeah, and he took Manuel by surprise and dragged him into the alley."

As often as Liz had visualized the killing, talk of it still made her shudder. "Even with my vivid imagination, I find it hard to picture Ramon being so jealous that he'd commit such a vicious murder," she said.

"You're not the only one. Ramon came across as a breed apart from a typical gang member. He must have worked hard on that image. The nurses and doctors in the hospital, and even the cops and detectives in the other precinct knew he was a Zuma, yet they all found him very likable. They were stunned when the truth came out."

"Besides being in a jealous rage, do you think he might have been *on* something when he set out to murder Manuel?"

"I guess it's possible, but according to the narcs, most dealers aren't users. They rake in the dough from their addicted clients and spend it on fancy cars and other luxuries."

"Did Ramon admit hiding his Mercedes in the alley and waiting for Manuel to come along?"

"That's another angle we had to work on. With his attorney present, he claimed he was nowhere near that alley the night of the murder. But when we told him about his prints on the C-note, he changed his story before the attorney could stop him. He admitted he'd confronted Manuel that night—on the street, not in the alley, and he said he was on foot. He said he never would have driven his Mercedes into Serps territory."

"And of course he denied stabbing Manuel."

"Yeah, he said he only wanted Manuel to promise he'd break up with Dolores, but when Manuel refused, they got into a fistfight that spilled over into the alley. He claimed Manuel threw the first punch, and after a couple of blows, he KO'ed Manuel."

"And while Manuel was knocked out, Ramon went through his pockets and found the birthday card?"

"Right. He admitted taking the bill from the birthday card, but he insisted that Manuel was unconscious but alive when he left him there in the alley. He must have been found and stabbed later on, he said. He suggested it might have been the Serps."

"A jury might think that sounded believable."

"Yeah. That's why we didn't stop with finding his prints and Gina's on the bill. We knew we had to prove he'd hidden his car in the alley and waited there for Manuel to pass by on his way home."

Liz nodded. That would indicate a premeditated attack. But from what Ike had said, he and Lou didn't know for sure that the Mercedes had been driven into the alley. How could they get Ramon to admit that?

"Ramon kept insisting he never would have driven his Mercedes into Serps territory," Ike continued. "But the fact that he'd lied about confronting Manuel and then changed his story made us believe he was lying about that too. To build a solid homicide case, we had to establish that he'd pulled the car into the alley and ambushed Manuel. When we told him the tire tracks in the alley matched the tire treads on his Mercedes, he broke down and admitted the car had been in the alley."

"Wait a minute," Liz said. "You told me all about the fingerprint testing. How come you've been holding out on me about running tests on tires and treads?"

"Don't get your Irish up. No tests were run. We were bluffing."

Bluffing? Liz was about to ask him why those tests on the tire marks and treads hadn't been run, when the answer came to her in a flash. Whatever tire impressions had been left in the dust and grime of the alley the night of the murder would have vanished with the blizzard's melting snow.

"You're so damn smart," she said, squeezing his hand. "Clever as Ramon is, he didn't pick up on the fact that the blizzard would have erased all traces of tire tracks."

"Fortunately, neither did his attorney," Ike replied. "And, faced with what he believed was irrefutable evidence, Ramon changed his story again. He admitted he'd hidden the car in the alley and taken Manuel by surprise when he walked by. He also admitted stabbing Manuel but claimed it was in self-defense."

"What's going to happen to him?" Liz asked.

"The DA wants to go for murder one, but last I heard, the attorney was going to negotiate a plea bargain. Whichever way it goes, it will be a long time before Ramon Otero is out and driving around in his Montezuma Mercedes."

"The Ruiz family must be feeling a great sense of relief," Liz said.

"Yeah. As soon as we were sure, Lou and I went to their home and told them. Of course it won't be over until after the trial, but at least this gave them some sense of closure."

"But it must be a terrible shock for Dolores and her mother."

Ike nodded. "It's always rough on a killer's relatives."

He'd seen many like Dolores and her mother, Liz thought—innocent people devastated by crimes committed by their family members. "And it must be especially painful for Dolores," she said. "Poor little girl, she has lost her sweetheart and also the boy she loved as a brother."

But their last hours in their honeymoon paradise should not be spent in grim discussion, she decided. Tightening her hand with Ike's, she said, "No more homicide talk. For the short time we have left of our honeymoon, let's forget about murders. We'll have enough of them after we get back to New York."

"Are you sure you can hold out that long?" he asked with a teasing grin.

She laughed. "Are you saying I'm hooked on homicides, and I'll need a fix before we get home?"

"Not exactly, but knowing you as well as I do, I've noticed you're never happier than when you have your teeth into a baffling murder. But that's one of the many things I love about you."

They paused for a kiss.

"But if you're sure you want to forget about homicides until we're back in New York, let's concentrate on getting some more photos before we head for the hotel to pack," Ike said.

He glanced toward a small grove of trees near the café. "How about a shot of you over there?"

"Okay, and then I'll take one of you."

Approaching the grove, they noticed a man wearing swim trunks and a white T-shirt stretched out on a chaise. A wine carafe and a goblet, both empty, stood on an adjacent table.

"We need more shots of us together," Ike said. "I'm going to ask that guy if he'd mind being a photographer for a few minutes."

"Oh, he looks like he's asleep," Liz said as they drew nearer. "We'd better not disturb him."

She'd barely spoken when she gasped and clutched Ike's arm.

He glanced at her with a quizzical smile. "What?"

She gestured toward the man on the chaise. "Look! There's blood on the front of his shirt. He's been stabbed in the chest! He's not asleep—he's *dead!*"

Frowning, Ike stepped closer to the chaise and bent over it. When, after a moment, he turned around, Liz was startled to see a grin on his face.

"That's not blood on his shirt—it's red wine. And, judging from his breath, he drank plenty of it before he passed out."

Their laughter must have penetrated the man's consciousness. He stirred, but they didn't wait to see if he opened his eyes. Like two mischievous children, they turned and fled.

Near the hotel's entrance, Ike caught her to him in a hug. "Good thing our plane's leaving in a couple of hours," he said. "I need to get you home before Redlocks Rooney stumbles upon a *real* murder."

"Correction," she replied. "Remember, I'm not keeping my maiden name. It's Redlocks Eichle, now."

He shook his head. "Pleased as I am that you want to take my name, Redlocks Eichle doesn't sound right."

She pondered that for a moment. "I agree, it doesn't have the same ring to it," she said. "So, in everyday life I'll be Mrs. George Eichle or Mrs. 'Ike' Eichle or Liz Eichle, but—"

He broke in with a laugh and a hug. "But when it comes to a very special part of our life together, you'll be what you've always been—my Redlocks Rooney."